PRAISE FOR
RON FAUST

"Faust's prose is as smooth and bright as a sunlit mirror."
—Publishers Weekly

"Hemingway is alive and well and writing under the name Ron Faust."
—Ed Gorman, author of *Night Kills*

"Faust is one of our heavyweights . . . you can't read a book by Ron Faust without the phrase 'major motion picture' coming to mind."
—Dean Ing, *New York Times* bestselling author of *The Ransom of Black Stealth One*

"Faust writes of nature and men like Hemingway, with simplicity and absolute dominance of prose skills."
—Bill Granger, award-winning author of *Hemingway's Notebook*

"He looms head and shoulders above them all—truly the master storyteller of our time. Faust will inevitably be compared to Hemingway."
—Robert Bloch, author of *Psycho*

THE LONG COUNT

RON FAUST

TURNER

Turner Publishing Company
200 4th Avenue North • Suite 950 • Nashville, Tennessee 37219
445 Park Avenue • 9th Floor • New York, New York 10022

www.turnerpublishing.com

THE LONG COUNT

This is a work of fiction. All the characters and events portrayed in
this book are either products of the author's imagination or are used
fictitiously.

Cover design: Glen M. Edelstein
Book design: Glen M. Edelstein

Library of Congress Catalog-in-Publishing Data
Faust, Ron.
  The long count / Ron Faust.
    pages ; cm.
  ISBN 978-1-62045-430-5
  I. Title.
  PS3556.A98L66 2013
  813'.54--dc23
                                            2013005050

Printed in the United States of America
13 14 15 16 17 18 19 0 9 8 7 6 5 4 3 2 1

PART ONE
QUITASOL

ONE

I killed a boy in the old bullring at Quitasol.

He really died that night in the bullring, but it took three weeks for his heart to quit. He was a game kid. His name was Cesar Caceras, he was twenty-two years old, and the newspapers claimed that he'd had a great future. He never emerged from the coma. Tubes fed him and tubes eliminated his wastes, and his hands were strapped to the bed frame because he had been clawing at his eyes while unconscious. The only words anyone heard him clearly speak before he died were, *"Mamá, qué quieres?"*

I was there along with his wife Elena, their son Jesús, his mother and father, and half a dozen other relatives. His mother began to weep and say her rosary when the comatose Cesar asked, "Mama, what do you want?"

His father, a hairy, barrel-torsoed *mestizo*, turned and started shadow-boxing in the corner of the hospital room. The newspapers said that he had taught Cesar to fight. When the man finally lowered his fists and turned again, I could see that he had been crying too.

I never saw Cesar's wife pray or recite the rosary or weep. After her husband was hurt she ceased being a Catholic and reverted to being Quechua. She waited and waited, as you see Indians waiting all over this continent, alongside roads, in the fields and shabby villages, everywhere. They have been waiting for many hundreds of years. It seems that they've forgotten the purpose of their long vigil. Maybe the missing entity is still en route and they will awaken to greet it. Or maybe it has already come and gone and they are really not waiting anymore, but are simply absorbed in listening to the echo of receding footsteps.

Elena looked like one of the clay figurines that you sometimes find in the *altiplano*. She had the same earth-colored skin and the same muddy brown eyes and the same quality of stolid, almost mindless waiting. She was the only member of the family who spoke to me. And I remember that on the day before Cesar died she brought me a paper cup of water from the cooler in the corridor.

On the day Cesar died, his father hit me. I saw it coming. He was powerful, like Cesar, and slow like Cesar, and just before the impact I snapped my head back, reducing the force of the blow, and I fell to the floor. I pretended to be stunned. I knew that I would have to get up and fight if he started kicking me; but it seemed that all that remained of his strength and rage had gone into that one punch. He turned and walked away. His dreams, his hope to imprint himself on the world, had died with his son.

I spent four hours a day, six days a week in the hospital with the unconscious Cesar and his family. It was always hot and stuffy, there were clay pots filled with withered flowers, flies walked on the walls and ceiling, women monotonously prayed, and Cesar's father shadow-boxed and furtively wept in the corner of the room.

I hated that room. God, how I loathed that three-week deathwatch over a still-breathing man. I went there six days a week because the people of the city expected it of me. No, they demanded it. And, too, I suppose I went there because I knew that if Cesar ever surfaced into momentary lucidity he would—not forgive, I didn't need that—he would *recognize* me. He would look at me in a certain way. He was a fighter. I would have done the same for him. God and family would have to wait while I acknowledged the man who had destroyed me.

The police confiscated my passport "pending the completion of their investigation." I did not know what they proposed to investigate. Nearly twenty thousand people had seen me kill Caceras in the ring, and there were the films. But there were rumors too; something about my gloves, the referee, the judges, treachery in Cesar's corner, American gangsters, a complete paranoid litany. The boxing world in the United States is psychotic; in Latin America it is demoniacal. And it seems that every Latin American male is engaged in a fierce witch-hunt against dishonor. Somehow, the fact that a thirty-six-year-old washed-up *gringo* pug had not only beaten but killed their *simpático* future champion of the world was intolerable. They had been dishonored. The nation had been dishonored. It began to seem as if only my blood could purify the Republic.

Newspapers called me the "poisoned opportunity." I was formally challenged to duel. There were many threats. A businessman tried to run me over with his car. A shoeshine boy spat in my face. Someone slashed the tires of my rented car. They hated me.

But every morning at dawn, while the sun was still timid and mist rose from the cobblestone streets, I would drive out beyond the paranoid rat-maze of the city and go running. On Sundays I packed a rucksack with food and water and a light sleeping bag and stayed out until Monday morning. I ran through the mountains like a demented hermit or an Indian courier of the old days. I was not in training anymore, but the habits of twenty years drove me on: my heart, lungs, and legs commanded me to run; they hardly cared that there was no longer any purpose in it. The body does not retire as easily as the mind. I ran up through the terraced fields and the farmers leaned on their hoes as they watched me; up into the grassy foothills, scattering herds of goats; on up into the *atmosfero raro*, sometimes past slowly plodding alpinists; up to the terminal moraines of glaciers—if I had owned crampons and an ice axe I might have hurried all the way to the summits. I was in superb physical condition, the best of my life. I was thirty-six years old. I had lost some speed, the quick snap of my reflexes, strength, but I had more stamina than ever before. And so I ran.

TWO

There was an open-air restaurant on the roof of the old Hotel Cristóbal Colón. They served a $7.95 steak for $13.95; you paid an extra six dollars for a view of the stars and, on nights of the new or full moon, an eerily luminous panorama of the snow-capped volcanoes south of the city. A hunchbacked pianist faked Gershwin and Cole Porter; candles guttered in the cool mountain breeze, and the white tablecloths seemed to levitate in the darkness; waiters flambéed everything that failed to move. At dusk, bats came out of the belfry of the church across the street and hunted insects over the tables. You could hear the faint squeaking of the bats and sometimes feel the shuddering breath of their wings.

Nine days after Caceras died, I was sitting at a table by the parapet with my South American manager, Nacho Carmona. Nacho, a Colombian, had been a very good lightweight boxer in the States during the late forties and early fifties, as quick and bloodthirsty as a weasel. He'd been lightweight champion for five months but then had lost the title during his first defense. After retiring, he'd made himself available to American fighters who needed guidance on their South American tours. I hired Nacho when I decided to come out of retirement. He took thirty percent off the top, but he had all the contacts, he knew whom to bribe and whom to trust and whom to avoid altogether: he was a dishonest man, but he was dishonest on *my* side, and he had survived in a milieu that would have defeated the Borgias.

Nacho would not permit me to enter the ring until our share of the gate was safely banked; he hired a competent physician to attend me at ringside, not a self-taught abortionist from the *barrio;* he trained me himself, making certain that I was in shape and prepared for each fight—Nacho babied me the same way you'd baby the last five thousand miles out of an old car. We both made money. We weren't friends, but we'd probably send each other Christmas cards for five or ten years.

He looked grotesque in the candlelight. He was a dried-up, bony little man with protuberant eyes, and patches of hair, like thistles, on a nearly bald head.

The waiter took our orders, shrimp cocktails, rare steaks, salads, and a bottle of red wine, and then Nacho leaned over the table and said, "Your shadow is here."

"I know. I saw him."

"Does he have a room in the hotel?"

"I think he sleeps in the lobby."

"Are you going to buy his dinner tonight?" Nacho spoke English swiftly, grammatically, but he usually accented the wrong syllables and so his staccato speech sounded like a foreign language that you were just beginning to comprehend.

"What do you advise, Nacho?" I asked.

"I advise you to continue buying his meals and alcohol and cigars. And his women, if it comes to that."

"Okay."

My shadow—his name was Emilio Durán—was the police agent who had been assigned to follow me after the Caceras fight. He was a fat, sweaty, sorrowful man of about fifty. His shirt collar was always dirty and there was never a crease in his trousers. Nacho had told me to pick up his checks under the theory that a well-fed, half-drunk expense-account profiteer would write friendly reports about me to his superiors.

Now I looked across the terrace, caught his glance, nodded and smiled.

He dipped his head toward me and raised his wine glass, thanking me in advance for buying his meal. I drank some water.

The waiter brought our drinks, a blend of fruit juices for Nacho and a Pisco sour for me.

Nacho picked some imaginary lint off his sport coat. "I can get you a fight," he said.

Can you?

"Yes. A good one."

"Stop harassing me, Nacho."

"One more fight, baby. Just one more."

"No more fights for me. None."

"I was on the telephone all afternoon. I can get you Barboa here, in five weeks."

Barboa was a Brazilian heavyweight and was ranked seventh in the world by the WBA.

"He'd kill me in a regular fight," I said. "He carried me through the exhibition match. You know that."

"We could fill the soccer stadium," Nacho said. "The bullring is too small to contain all the people who would come out to see you get hurt."

"Barboa would take me out in two or three rounds. Sixty thousand people would riot, lynch me, burn down the stadium, and loot the city."

"No," Nacho said. "I don't think so."

"Yes," I said. "I think so."

"Barboa would carry you for five or six rounds. And then the first time he hit you hard you could fall down."

"This is crazy. You're crazy, Nacho."

"I can arrange the fight if you want it."

"I don't want it."

"You're in shape. You're stuck in this country for a while. The money you've earned during the last eight months is dribbling away. You could buy an automobile on what you'll end up spending on that fat cop over there."

"No," I said. "Thanks but no."

"The first time Barboa pins you with that left hook of his, fall down."

"I would anyway."

"Sixty thousand people would leave the stadium happy. The government would ease up on you. You could go home in prosperous humiliation."

"Did you ever take a dive, Nacho?"

"Twice. I got two good offers."

"Look, I know Barboa can beat me. If I was twenty-six years old, he couldn't. I'd win. I know he's too much for me now, and I'd like to be able to fall down, collect my money, and go home, but I can't. I just can't do it. My mind might agree, but I know that my body would become defiant at the crucial moment. I'd keep getting up and Barboa would keep knocking me down again. I'd get hurt."

"You're not that tough. Believe me, if Barboa pins you good you won't get up."

"Okay. But the answer is still no."

"Fifty thousand dollars and a percentage of the gate."

"You didn't mention the percentage before, Nacho."

"I have no agreement on a percentage, but I'm sure I can get the percentage."

"How much money are we talking about now?"

"I'll have to talk to Barboa's people."

"Nacho, if I should happen to receive notice that seventy-five thousand dollars has been deposited to an account in my name in the Bahamas . . . "

"You'll fight him?"

"Yes."

"You want seventy-five thousand clear?"

"Right. And I'll worry about the IRS."

"Maybe," he said. "Just possibly . . . I'll try."

Bats were performing aerobatics in the darkness that hovered above the candlelight. The lights of the city and the stars overhead seemed to be reflections of each other. The moon was rising and the snowy cones of the volcanoes began to emerge out of the darkness, glowing with a greenish-white phosphorescence.

"One more payday," Nacho said. "And then quit. Don't come out of retirement again."

Time often seems to hesitate in the few brief moments which separate twilight from full night. It is similar to those occasions when your heart breaks rhythm, contracts and is silent (you listen, waiting), and then suddenly it leaps in your chest and time resumes. It was like that now. I became aware that I could no longer hear the sounds of traffic in the street below, the cries of vendors, the angry shouts of children playing soccer in the vacant lot behind the church, the dull clink of utensils against plates here in the restaurant.

The hunchbacked pianist was now studying a sheet of music. The people on the terrace, including Nacho and myself, reminded me of figures in old photographs or Impressionist paintings: the models all dead, cold, and gone, but still fragmentally preserved in attitudes of eating and drinking and laughing. We were all, it seemed to me, simultaneously unborn, living, and dead. I saw myself from the grave and was surprised. I appeared to be a happy man. But how could that be? I had not (I thought of myself in the past tense for an instant) been happy then.

A horn blasted in the street below us. The hunchback began to play *Rhapsody in Blue* as if it were a military march. "They treat you like cattle," an elderly blue-haired American woman at a nearby table said. "Swine," the old man with her said. "Not cattle, swine."

"Here are the shrimp cocktails," Nacho said. "Are you going to buy my dinner?"

"Yes."

"Fool. I told you to watch your money."

"I'll start now."

"No, start after you pay this check."

After dinner Nacho went off to the Café Bolsa, where the fight crowd congregated, and I took the elevator to my room on the fourth floor. I made a gin and tonic and carried it out onto the small balcony. Cars crawled along the dark street below like incandescent-eyed beetles. There was a smell of rain in the air. The lights of the city were dully reflected off the clouds.

I did not believe that Nacho would succeed in arranging a fight with Barboa; that had been mostly hopeful speculation, an idea of his that had turned into a wish and then a certainty. That was how the fight business worked, or failed to work; only about one of five proposed matches ever reached the ring. But if Nacho was able to put all the pieces together, and the money was right, I would willingly remain here for another couple of months.

Barboa was damned tough. I had fought a three-round exhibition match with him in Rio de Janeiro the winter before. It had taken place in a huge seafront nightclub. The ring had been erected in the center of the dining room. The front circle of tables had been moved well back so that the men's white dinner jackets and the ladies' long gowns would not be spattered with blood and sweat. Candles glowed on the tables, an orchestra played *bossa nova* between rounds, and nearly two hundred men and women enjoyed a splendid dinner while the fighters hit each other.

A pair of good young welterweights fought as the cocktails and canapés were served; Barboa and I were the main course, so to speak; and two tough middle-weights bloodied each other after dessert, while the ladies were in the powder room or strolling in the garden, and the men relaxed with cognac and cigars.

It was a strange experience for me, a shock of opposites, like the indiscriminate blending of two dissimilar dreams. I could smell food and expensive perfumes while Barboa and I boxed, hear the muted dinner-table conversations and the occasional clink of a utensil, as in any good restaurant. The diners did not encourage us; there were no cheers, groans, whistles, insults—just the refined silence and a little polite applause after the round. And then the orchestra began to play.

The other fighters, having something to prove and gain, fought hard. Barboa and I coasted through the three rounds. Without speaking of it, without even exchanging a glance, we had tacitly agreed to not play zoo animals for the amusement of the diners.

And so we put on a demonstration of boxing skill. We showed them that boxing could be an athletic contest of the highest order, as valid as any sport. We employed all the knowledge and technique and natural gifts that we possessed, but we pulled our punches at the last instant. At first we were like two master fencers fighting a duel with rubber-tipped foils; and then, as we learned the other's style and rhythm, it became almost like a dance. We moved, we sparred, we took turns on offense and defense, we threw our best combinations, but so skillfully that our skin was not even reddened at the end of the third round. Barboa and I had thoroughly enjoyed the exhibition, but the diners did not seem to appreciate it; they had, of course, paid a great deal of money to witness acts of violence, not a ballet.

It started to rain lightly. I went into the room and mixed another drink. I felt like getting drunk. Why not? I was an ex-athlete now. I phoned the desk and asked the clerk to send up a bottle of gin, two bottles of tonic, and some limes. When the bellboy arrived with the items I asked him if he could get me a girl. Of course, he said. A pretty girl? Certainly. Clean? He was offended. Of course, of course, they are all government inspected.

THREE

The boxing match had originally been scheduled for Saturday, but there had been a heavy rain that morning, and so I fought Caceras at nine o'clock on Sunday night. A bullfight had taken place that afternoon and I could smell the bitter metallic blood-and-viscera stink from the *desolladero*—the butcher's shed beneath the grandstands. The butchers, clad in raincoats, drained and quartered the bulls as soon as they had been dragged from the arena. Now a few starving dogs prowled the shed, stopping here and there to lick the cement floor.

Nacho was kneading my shoulder and back muscles. "How do you feel?" he asked.

"I'm okay."

Just inside the *cuadrilla* gate there was a small chapel where the bullfighters prayed before entering the arena. Caceras spent a few moments praying before a statue of the Virgin while photographers took his picture from the doorway. There were more than one hundred people milling about; reporters, photographers, local fighters and managers and promoters and their entourages, big-eyed children, spectators down from the grandstands to look us over before placing their bets, drink and food vendors who refilled their trays from the concession shacks. Above our heads, the grandstands vibrated from the weight and movement of the crowd.

It was a hot, brutally humid night; the air was heavy and sheet lightning rolled across the sky like the surf on a stormy sea. There was a tension in the air, a mood of gathering violence, as twenty thousand individuals gradually welded themselves into a single great beast. I was not afraid of Caceras, but the Latin American crowds frightened me: if they became displeased they might riot, throw bottles and chairs into the ring, draw their revolvers (a great many Latin American men carried guns), attack the fighters and the officials and the police and each other. I expected to defeat Caceras; I did not expect to be declared the winner. The referee, the judges, and especially the crowd would not permit it. Caceras was the hometown boy, their idol, the "future champion of the world." I would win, Caceras would be credited with the victory, and everyone would be happy, including me, because this was a big payday and the last fight of my career.

Caceras emerged from the small chapel, saw me, shook his head and smiled. His smile was a generous act, a signal that united us while excluding everyone else participating in this vulgar carnival. We understand, his smile told me, we respect each other; what these thousands of fools think and say and do really has no relevance. I nodded and raised my gloves, thumbs up. He winked and turned away. We fought for money, but we could just as easily go into an empty gym and box for sport, as two men will oppose each other in tennis or handball.

Two red-jacketed flunkeys unbolted and then slowly swung open the heavy gates. I followed two policemen out onto the firmly packed grayish sand of the arena and then stopped, momentarily blinded by the lights. *"Ándale,"* Nacho said. I started down the narrow aisle and into the throbbing blast of crowd noise. Whistles, stamping feet, applause, shrill *macho* cries, all blended together in an animal roar that dried my mouth and tightened my scalp. Faces, distorted with emotion, were isolated and disembodied by the lights . . . satyrs, gargoyles, vampires, zombies, an assembly of monsters.

The stadium was filled. Folding chairs had been erected on the arena sand from the red fence all the way to ringside. The encircling bowl was a blurred, shifting mass of color that seemed to tremble and surge, expand and contract. I was glad that the ring had been located in the center; the grandstand crowd could not throw cups of urine down on our heads, as they did to some bullfighters who approached too close to the perimeter of the ring.

I climbed the portable wooden steps and entered the ring between the top and middle ropes. The crowd roared, wave after wave of noise that I could actually feel on my skin. I had never fought before so rabidly enthusiastic a crowd. They did not seem hostile toward me: Cesar was their boy, they loved him, but they did not yet hate me. In fact, I believe that the majority of the crowd liked me at that moment; I was a name fighter down from the States, a refugee from the big time, and whatever *cartel* I had earned throughout the years would belong to Cesar after he beat me. Young warriors acquire their reputations by defeating old warriors.

Now Cesar entered the ring, and the plaza crowd exploded. The noise changed pitch, rose higher, still higher, until it became like a scream. My ears hurt.

The public-address announcer introduced us in Spanish:

"From the United States of America, weighing two hundred and twelve pounds, Jim Racine." (He pronounced my name "Heem Rah-*ceen*-eh.")

"From Quitasol, *Quitasol*, of the great Republic of—" and the crowd's roar submerged the remainder of the introduction.

We met in the center of the ring to receive the instructions. I scraped my shoe soles on the rosin-dusted canvas; Caceras shrugged his shoulders and tapped his gloves together. We covertly studied each other, looking, glancing away, looking again. His face was badly beat up for so young a fighter; his nose was flattened in the center, one ear was beginning to cauliflower, there were old, slick white scars on his cheekbones and the bones above his eyes, and I could see some newer, pink-lipped scar tissue from a fight he'd had two months ago. He had won that fight, but he'd taken a lot of punches. Cesar was easy to hit. He was five foot ten, four inches shorter than I, with heavily muscled arms and legs and a thick, hairy torso.

We touched gloves and returned to our corners.

Nacho was giving me his instructions, but I had heard it all before and I did not listen. I felt stupid, numbed, and I knew that I would continue to feel that way until the first time I got hit. Now all I noticed was that the lights had attracted a great many insects, moths with the wingspread of sparrows, mosquitoes, reddish-colored beetles, fireflies . . .

The bell, we met in the center of the ring, and Cesar immediately began stalking me. He fought from a crouch, always boring in, nearly defenseless himself, just waiting for the opportunity to unload his big right hand. He wasn't a boxer; he was a brawler of the bars-and-alleys style.

I jabbed, keeping him back on his heels, off balance; I retreated, circled, clinched, jabbed again. He was easy to hit. I had a longer reach and I was much faster, and I kept ripping him with the jabs, and sometimes I quickly followed the jab with a short left hook. His own left was just a pawing motion, almost a shove; there was no snap in it. He was even slower than he had looked in the films. We were both slick and gleaming with sweat halfway through the round. Just before the bell I snapped his head back with a good jab, and his perspiration formed a brief silver halo in the ring lights.

I sat down in my corner; someone removed my mouthpiece and Nacho sponged cool water over my head and shoulders.

"Jesus, Nacho," I said. "This man can't fight."

"He's better than this," Nacho said. "Be careful, he's much better than this."

"The man can't defend himself."

"I've seen him fight, he's strong, he can hit, stay away from him, don't try to slug it out."

The second and the third rounds went the same way; I hit Caceras, and hit him and hit him and hit him, and he kept coming. The skin of his face and upper torso were red from my blows. His nose was bleeding and I had opened a cut above his right eye. Now, when I hit him solidly, the sweat mist had a pinkish hue.

The canvas was slippery with sweat in some areas, and in the fourth round I slipped to one knee. The referee called it a knockdown and made me take the mandatory eight-count. Most of the crowd cheered; there were only a few whistles. Apparently Caceras himself believed that it had been a legitimate knockdown, for he recklessly charged me after the count and I stiffened him with a left jab, froze him for a moment, snapped his head to one side with a left hook, and then threw my best right hand. The air misted with sweat and blood. I forced him back against the ropes and hit him with alternating lefts and rights, street-brawler style. His eyes were dull and muddy. He expelled breath every time I hit him, "Huh! huh! huh!" The bell rang early. Nacho timed the round at two minutes and forty-three seconds. Cesar had friends everywhere.

I was dizzy from the heat and salt loss.

"Finish him this round," Nacho said. "Put him away."

"Nacho, the kid's hurt. They've got to stop it."

"They won't stop it. You know they can't."

"He's a sleepwalker."

"His last fight took too much out of him," Nacho said. "He should have waited six months, a year, before fighting again. Maybe he should have quit. Put him away. Get it over. The only way you can help him is to put him away."

Caceras was incapable of defending himself. I could hit him with any punch I chose, at any time. In the first minute I reopened the cut over his eye. His nose was streaming blood. We were both covered with his blood. Then I hit him harder than I've ever hit a man: his head snapped back and his mouthpiece flew across the ring. The air around him clouded with a bloody mist. His knees buckled and he slowly sank down toward the canvas, but then some insane instinct halted his fall, a courage that survived unconsciousness, and he slowly, so slowly, straightened his legs and was erect again. His hands were hanging at his sides. His eyes had rolled up-ward and all I could see were the bloody whites of his eyes. He had been knocked out, but his body refused to fall down.

I hit Caceras, not hard, and he went down onto his back. His legs flexed as if with severe cramps. The ref-eree gave him a slow count. He was down for at least fifteen seconds. He rolled over onto his chest, lay flat for a moment, rose to his hands and knees, collapsed, rose again, and then he somehow got to his feet.

He staggered like a drunk. I could not hit him again.

I sat down on my stool in the corner. It was raining lightly now. Lightning crackled overhead and rain pattered against the canvas of the ring.

"I'm not going to hit him anymore," I said.

"I'll stop it," Nacho said, and he threw a towel into the ring.

We would forfeit the match: we could tell the press that I was sick, injured, anything. But the referee hooked his toe beneath the towel and kicked it out into the crowd.

I did not hit Caceras during the next round. He tottered after me like a drunk, or an infant, or a very old man. Lightning ripped open the sky and the silver rain streaked down through the lights, and silver pellets leaped off the canvas. Cesar stalked me and then suddenly he straightened, his eyes wide, he wavered, his body still fighting long after his brain had surrendered, and he fell forward like a tree.

The crowd was silent now. Perhaps they were confused by the sudden rain. But they did not move for shelter. They sat quietly in the seats and did not file toward the exits until after Caceras had been taken away on a stretcher.

FOUR

I visited the American consulate and was told that there was nothing they could do to help me unless I were arrested and jailed; then I would receive weekly visits from one of the staff, who would try to insure that I did not receive worse treatment than the imprisoned nationals.

I said: "Do you mean that you people can't provide any help unless I'm put in jail?"

"Well, basically, yes," the young vice-consul said. He was about twenty-three years old and he had apple cheeks and eyes that looked at you sideways, sadly, as if he had just been beaten or expected to be beaten soon.

"Then, if I'm jailed, you'll help me by asking the authorities not to beat or starve me more than the other prisoners?"

"I wouldn't put it quite that way," said the vice-consul, smiling.

"Well, how would you put it?"

"I'm sorry, but there's really nothing we can do at this time."

"What if it's the practice of a particular government to blind all of its prisoners? Does that mean you can't protest if an American is also blinded?"

"That's absurd," he said.

"I just want to get this straight."

"Mr. Racine, please, I'm very busy."

"You were working a crossword puzzle when I came into this office. How can you be busy when it seems that all you have to do is make sure the same model thumbscrew is used on all prisoners regardless of national origin?"

"Mr. Racine, this is nonsense."

"Is it? Aren't you aware that prisoners in this country are tortured?"

"That's an exaggeration, I'm sure."

"How can you exaggerate the fact of torture?"

"Really, there's nothing we can do. I understand your disappointment."

"I'm not disappointed, I'm angry."

"Oh, well, I'm afraid your anger won't accomplish a thing."

"What would you do, Mr. Vice-Consul, if the imprisoned nationals are stretched out on the rack and the imprisoned Americans are staked out on an anthill?"

"This is ridiculous."

"It certainly is."

The vice-consul began rearranging papers on his desk. His face was very red.

"What would you do if there were weevils in my bread and only mold on the bread of a national?"

"Mr. Racine . . . "

"What if they pulled off my fingernails, and only pulled off the toenails of the nationals?"

"Good day, Mr. Racine."

"Where are the gunboats, Mr. Vice-Consul?"

He took a sheet of paper from his IN basket, read it quickly, scrawled his initials at the bottom, and then placed it in the OUT basket.

I leaned over and removed the paper from the basket. The vice-consul tried to grab my wrist, but he was too slow.

"I want to see what it is that keeps you foreign-service chaps so busy," I said.

"That is private, Mr. Racine."

"Top secret?

"That is private government business, Mr. Racine. You could get in a great deal of trouble."

"I'm already in trouble," I said. "What do I have to fear from you? You've admitted that you're powerless in this country."

He picked up the telephone, paused a moment, drumming his pencil on the desk, then said, "Marie, send in the guards, please."

The paper said that all who expected to attend the annual American Diplomatic Corps picnic at Vista-hermosa should initial this memo. The embassy staff, the consulate staff, and many prominent members of the American business community had been invited. There would be fine food and beverages, native entertainment, swimming, softball, tennis, golf, games and prizes for the children, and FUN FUN FUN for all.

The guards entered the room.

I stood up. The vice-consul's face was very red, almost purplish-red, now, and he did not look at me.

The guards escorted me out of the building.

There had been some terrorist activity in the country and so security was tight at the U.S. Embassy. The Marine guards checked my papers and had me pass through a metal detector before I was permitted to go through the tall, spear-tipped iron gates. The embassy looked like an old, sprawling Spanish villa; it had white stucco walls, red roof tiles, and tall, deeply set windows. There were flagstone walks, wooden benches beneath the flowering hibiscus trees, and a small lake upon which swans glided like exiled nobles.

The ambassador did not have time to see me. I returned many times, and I talked to clerks and more clerks and finally to the ambassador's private secretary. The ambassador did not have time to see me even though during the days while I waited he had time to see American tractor salesmen, oil-company geologists, a ballet company from California, a pair of alpinists, the captain of a U.S. basketball team, and many prosperous-looking American tourists.

I finally managed to obtain an interview with the ambassador's secretary, Miss Alicia Phillips. She was in her late twenties, tall and poised, with ash-blonde hair and cool blue eyes and a drawling, beautifully modulated Southern accent—a Virginia accent, I thought. I had overheard gossip while hanging around the Embassy. One of the clerks called her the ambassador's "Phillips screw."

"I'm sorry the ambassador wasn't able to see you today, Mr. Racine," she said when I was seated in her office.

"He hasn't been able to see me for quite a number of days," I replied.

"He's a very busy man, as I'm sure you understand."

"He goes golfing three or four afternoons a week."

Her eyes and her voice cooled a little. "Important diplomatic affairs can be settled on the golf course and at cocktail parties as well as in the office," she said.

"Get me an invitation to a cocktail party, then. Or golf—hell, I play golf."

"Mr. Racine, I'm familiar with your problem. What is it that you wish the ambassador to do?"

"Get this government to return my passport to me. I want to go home."

"Well, it's hardly as easy as that."

"I'm sure it is."

"You're mistaken."

"Look, all the ambassador has to do is pick up his telephone and call one of his chums and I can be out of this country within twenty-four hours."

"Oh, Mr. Racine," she said, smiling. "Things simply do not work that way."

"Of course they do. We both know they work that way. That's the way everything works—a chum picking up the phone and confidentially talking to a chum. That's even what the presidential hot line is all about; so the big chums can talk things over after the little chums have fouled things up."

"The ambassador would be interfering in the internal affairs of a foreign government."

"Miss Phillips, do I look like a moron? For Christ's sake, it is the *duty* of diplomats to coax, persuade, threaten, bribe, to interfere."

She smiled. "Mr. Racine, you *are* difficult."

"I'm in a difficult situation."

"I've read a report on the matter," she said. "And it seems to me that the Caceras boy *did* die under unusual circumstances."

"He was beaten to death," I said.

She was confused by my bluntness.

"I killed him with my fists. Those are highly unusual circumstances at a cocktail party or on the sixteenth green, but not in the ring."

"Yes. Well, I'm sure you must feel terrible about it."

"I'm not here for sympathy."

"Mr. Racine, as I understand it, there is now an investigation of the incident in progress. I'm sure that as soon as it's completed you'll be permitted to return to America."

"The odds are in my favor," I said.

"Well, then?" She smiled charmingly.

"Well, if you're wrong I'll go to jail."

"Oh, no, certainly not. Not if you're innocent of any wrongdoing."

I stared at her.

She was smiling at me.

"Do you mean, Miss Phillips, that the pure in heart shall not suffer?"

"Be patient, Mr. Racine."

"I can see that you aren't going to help me."

"It seems to me that you are not yet in need of our help."

"Okay," I said.

"But keep us informed. Really," she said, "I'm certain that everything will work out."

"It will for you. You have diplomatic immunity."

She laughed.

"The embassy—I'm on American soil, right?"

"Yes."

"What if I refuse to leave?"

She laughed again.

"What would you do if I refused to leave the grounds?"

"I know you're teasing, Mr. Racine."

"This is United States soil, my country. Hypothetically—"

"Why," she said gaily, "if you refused to leave I would call the Marine guards."

I rose from my chair.

"You don't look like a boxer," she said.

"No?"

"Except, maybe, for the scar tissue around your eyes."

I did not reply.

"And maybe your nose."

"The nose has been changed a little."

"You don't talk like a boxer, either."

"How is that?"

"Oh, you know." She smiled.

"Have you known many boxers?" I asked.

"No," she said. "But you don't speak as one expects a fighter to speak."

"You mean I don't talk as if my mouth was filled with blood and broken teeth."

She laughed. It was a gay, softly musical laugh, almost a song. She was a pretty Southern girl, schizophrenic in the Southern-belle way; warming you up and then freezing you, alternately icy, coquettish, sulking, joyful, sweetly sad, running your emotions up and down like a yo-yo. Good, clean Baptist girl, scented of starch and lilac, a sanctified clarity in the eyes, but you were always subtly made aware that somewhere, deep down, if only you could reach that far, was a crazy heated whore . . . broken promises.

"Thank you," I said.

"Come back and see me," she said. "Any time."

I went to see one of the most successful lawyers in the city. Dr. *Licenciado* Jorge Silveta wore a tight black Italian suit, kangaroo-hide shoes with gold buckles, half-dollar-sized cufflinks, a silk ascot in the national colors, and insect-eye sunglasses. He played here's-the-church-here's-the-steeple with his hands while I told him my story.

"I see," he said. "Yes."

"Perhaps you could expedite matters."

He twisted his hands and lo! the church doors opened and there were all the people. He watched them with distaste for a moment and then dismantled the church and hid all the people in his armpits.

"Yes, yes," he said. "But it will be expensive."

"How expensive?"

He studied me for a moment; I could see my twin reflections on the lenses of his sunglasses. "Three thousand dollars."

"How long would it take you to recover my passport?"

"Oh, perhaps a week. Ten days. No more than ten days, certainly."

I got out my checkbook. "May I borrow your pen?"

He passed his fountain pen over the desk. It was made out of a gold alloy, very heavy, with an ornate scrollwork of tiny monkeys and ferns and parrots. The desk itself was constructed out of heavy black mahogany, and the four legs pretended to be cherubs.

"I'll give you a third now as a retainer, and the rest when you hand me my passport."

"No, no," he said. "I must have all of it now."

"Why?"

"Well, you see, there are . . . *propinas*."

"You don't mean *propinas*, you mean *mordidas*. Bribes, not tips. Can you guarantee success, *Licenciado?*"

"Absolutely," he said.

"I'll give you half of the money now."

"No, I must have all of it."

"Have a good lunch with the hundred-dollar retainer I gave to your secretary," I said, and I threw his fountain pen on the desk and left the room. By the time I'd got on the elevator I had forgotten what he looked like; I remembered his clothing and jewelry and voice, but his face was now just a blurry smear in my memory. On nights of the full moon, the *licenciado* probably stripped off his clothes and ran with the coyotes.

FIVE

I continued to go up into the mountains during this period; it was the only way I knew to burn away my frustration and rage.

I had always assumed that the problem with the human race was simply our ignorance and stupidity, but now I began to suspect it was something else; perversity, a gratuitous, contrary meanness. We were like scorpions trapped together in a bottle, stinging each other and ourselves, even coming together in matings that were all too often deadly. There was a venom in us. I did not exclude myself: I was a man who had earned a great deal of money beating other men with my fists. I might even convert Caceras's death into a resort hotel in the sun.

Some encounters with the rural people diluted my bitterness a little. I liked many of them, the high-country farmers and herders. They were extremely poor, their lives were hard, and yet I found them more serene and far kinder than the people of the plains and cities. The harshness of their lives seemed to have purified them in a way, made them eccentric and sweet. I did not romanticize them. Poverty and ignorance and disease are not worthy of any kind of mystification. Still, they seemed to me to be good people; and I did not doubt and hate myself so much that I felt incapable of judging between good and bad—I intended to leave the peculiarly modern confusion to more sophisticated thinkers.

One afternoon an old goat herder and I shared our lunches. His summer camp was high above the valley, close to fifteen thousand feet, where patches of snow lasted from spring to autumn and the vegetation was so sparse that only goats could survive on it. The mountain slope was littered with glacial rubble, and his goat herd was actually grazing among the boulders of the terminal moraine. Above, I could see the white tongue of the glacier; below, a billowing sea of clouds. It was very hot in the sun, but when I sheltered in a wedge of shadow I became chilled. We were in the sky. The sky was all around us, below us.

He was a thin man with white hair and eyebrows and a tobacco-stained white moustache. His face and neck were deeply wrinkled, and when he smiled all the lines tightened and formed concentric whorls on his sun-blackened face.

We talked awkwardly in Spanish and then he invited me up to his cave. The dogs would not permit the goats to stray far, he said. He had goat's milk and cheese in the cave, and bread; he baked his own unleavened bread.

We scrambled up over the rocks to a small opening in the cliffside. He was old, perhaps in his mid-seventies, but he was accustomed to an outdoor life at this altitude and he was not even breathing hard when we reached the cave entrance.

The cave was small, forty feet long, fifteen feet wide, and no more than ten feet high. It was sparsely furnished: a few wooden crates, a goatskin bed on the stone floor, an old oil stove, pots and pans, some clothing, and a crucifix and some gaudily colored religious prints affixed to the wall.

There was a low, jagged tunnel opening at the rear of the cave.

"Does the cave go back much farther?" I asked.

"A little ways," he said. There's a big cave behind this one."

It seemed to me that caves here were a geological anomaly.

"How big is the cave?" I asked.

"As big as the cathedral in the city. Would you like to see it?"

"Are the candles bright enough to light the place?"

"Not very well," he said.

"Could I come back sometime with a good flashlight and explore the cave?"

"Certainly," he said. "But there really isn't much to see."

This cave was where he lived during the summer, he said. He had a stone house in the village below. His wife was dead. His children had long ago moved into the city. He had two fine, strong grandchildren, he said proudly, and they had been educated and could read and write and speak in foreign languages—"your language too, probably." They were very busy but sometimes they found time to visit him. They brought presents, a small radio once, but the batteries were dead now, otherwise we could listen to the music and voices from Quitasol. His children and grandchildren had taken him to live in the city years ago, but he could not breathe there, he didn't know why, his lungs had filled with fluid and he had been forced to return to the mountains. "These mountains," he said contemptuously. "Nothing but stones." Someday, when his lungs were healthy again, he would return to live in the city and watch television and go to the soccer matches and wear a black suit and sit in the *plaza mayor* and watch all the people. And church—they had a giant cathedral in the city, and the bishop himself sometimes gave communion; while down in the village they had a tiny stone church and the priest was so old and deaf that you had to shout during confession, and within half an hour all of your sins were the gossip of the community. What do you think of that? They know how to do things right in the city.

The old man loved to talk. He felt guilty for not going to live in the city with his children and grandchildren. "I even smell like a goat," he said with self-contempt. He was very happy. Guilt contributed to his happiness: the mountains, which he had taken for granted throughout his life, now had the new attraction of being vaguely shameful. His lungs were smarter than his family.

He provided goat's cheese and milk and unleavened bread; I had sausage, regular bread, two oranges, and a bottle of Chilean wine. The old man got drunk on his share of the wine.

We sat at the mouth of the cave, eating and drinking and talking, looking down to where the steep slope vanished into the clouds.

He wanted me to stay for dinner. He said he would kill a kid and roast it over an open fire—he had brought a couple bags of charcoal from the village. Was it true that men had walked on the moon? He didn't believe it. I told him no, that it had all been faked on the Arizona desert. He laughed, delighted with the wine and a conspiracy of knowledge. He had looked at the moon night after night in all of its phases, year after year, sometimes thinking yes, it may be, other times thinking no, it's nonsense. What a wonderful joke! A desert in *los Estados Unidos*—what was the name of the desert? Arizona? Arizona! What a hoax!

He enjoyed the wine so much that I gave him most of my share.

Stay, he said, we'll roast a whole kid and eat it out beneath the moon. He found the untrod moon hilarious.

I said that I was sorry, but that I had to return to the city.

"Well, here, take this, then."

He had carved some sort of fetish out of the tip of a ram's horn. It was small, yellowish, and slightly greasy to the touch, like ivory. It had been carved and then smoothly polished, but I could not recognize any animal in the form. It might have been a bird, a fox, a fish, anything. I did not ask what it represented; he acted as if I should know.

"Well . . . "

"It's so boring up here that sometimes I carve," he said shyly. "It's stupid, but the radio doesn't work anymore."

"It's very nice," I said.

"Can I keep the wine bottle?" he asked. "I can use it to store water."

"Of course you can have it."

"Do you like the animal?" he asked.

"Yes, I like it very much. Thank you." I gave him my pocketknife in return.

"The animal will bring you luck," he said. "When are you going to come back and explore the cave?"

"Next week," I said. "Is there anything I can bring you?"

"Wine," he said, laughing.

We said goodbye, and then I picked up my rucksack and started down over the rocks. The dogs barked at me. The herd of goats parted to let me through and then closed again. Before I reached the cloud I turned and saw, far above me, just a dot in the dark oval of the cave entrance, the old man. I waved and then descended into the mist.

SIX

On Sunday I crashed the U.S. Diplomatic Corps picnic at Vistahermosa. I intended to confront the ambassador and ask—*demand*—that he intervene on my behalf before I became buried in a manila folder in a green filing cabinet in a flyspecked office somewhere in the city. The inquiry into the death of Caceras, a red herring from the beginning, had now reached a state of bureaucratic stasis. Caceras was losing importance as new, equally insignificant affairs erupted to occupy the brains and hearts of government clerks. The policeman, Durán, no longer followed me. I was two-thirds forgotten now. It had required the order of someone in authority to initiate the investigation and forbid my exit from the country; it would require the same man, or another with equal power, to effect my release.

Vistahermosa was a nine-hundred-acre oasis thirty miles beyond the city limits. The land and the resort-hotel complex were owned by an American soft drink company. It all lay on the lower slopes of a twenty-thousand-foot-high volcano and was well irrigated by snow-melt from above; there were three creeks and one river running through the land, many ponds, and a series of smoking, rainbow-misted waterfalls. The final waterfall dropped ninety feet into a lake as clear and blue as any South Pacific lagoon. There were tennis and squash courts, two swimming pools, an eighteen-hole golf course, stables and bridle paths, and a polo field. About half of the nine hundred acres were kept in a semi-wild condition.

I paid the taxi driver, told him I would find my own way back to the city, and then I wandered around the grounds. A steer, two pigs, three lambs, and a kid were being spit-roasted in the wind-fluttering shade of some eucalyptus trees. Women greased with suntan lotion sat on blankets in the grass and scolded their small children, who ran and fell and cried. The older children, especially the boys, reminded me of quick, fierce predators; ferrets and margays and foxes.

I stopped to watch a father-son softball game (they, parents and offspring, seemed to hate each other), and later I walked over to the tennis courts to watch part of a match between the club pro and the embassy's assistant commercial attaché. I'd heard that the assistant attaché, a man named Dan Grogan, was the CIA's chief of station in this country. Grogan was a rangy, freckled, red-haired man of about thirty-five. He played tennis as though it were a vaudeville act: he laughed and clowned throughout the match, attracting and then amusing a crowd of spectators. He was very good. He had a powerful serve, a hard topspin forehand and an equally hard backhand slice. He chattered all the time in English, Spanish, and French, and he attempted trick shots that, when they succeeded, made the club pro look inept. The more points and games Grogan accumulated, the more cheerful he became. The pro was gloomy.

"Dan plays very well, don't you think?"

I turned. It was Alicia Phillips, the ambassador's secretary. Her ash-blonde hair looked almost white in the sun glare. Her eyes were a different color in the outdoor light too, less opaque, paler, almost a turquoise blue-green. She was taller than I remembered, about five-eight. Only her voice was the same, that lilting, seductive tone of the Southern belle.

"Yes," I said. "Grogan plays the game well."

"He was on the tennis team at USC," she said.

"He's a bully," I said.

"Dan?"

"He shouldn't humiliate the pro this way. It could cost the man his job, not to mention his pride."

"Oh, no, Dan's just playing and having fun."

"How much fun is the pro having now?"

"Well, never mind Dan. I see that you received my invitation to the picnic."

"Yes, thank you."

Tiny laugh lines gathered at the corners of her eyes. "I didn't send you an invitation," she said.

"That's the one I didn't receive."

"Do you know that you've been followed by one of our security men?"

"I saw him. He looks like a mortician. An unsuccessful mortician, out on a Sunday to drum up a little trade."

"You've been asking questions about the whereabouts of the ambassador."

"Yes. Surprise, he's golfing."

"There have been many threats on the ambassador's life. You are a stranger."

"Why has the ambassador been threatened? Doesn't he pay his golf debts?"

"You're naughty," she said, smiling.

It had been twenty years since a pretty girl called me naughty. I liked it. I also liked the way she touched my arm lightly, briefly; and how she stood close to me, close enough so that I could smell her soapy lilac scent. Some Southern girls are as skilled in attracting men as geishas are in pleasing them. I was not fooled by her belle manners and techniques (she was not interested in me); but I was pleased by her attention nevertheless. She activated something like magnetic fields between us. There was a touch of genuine mystery beneath her artifice. She was feminine in a way that is rare now. She was dishonest, yes, but I remembered the days when females were not just boys with a variation in plumbing, and I rather enjoyed this harmless flirting.

"You were a cheerleader," I said.

"I beg your pardon? Oh, why yes, I was."

"At the University of Virginia?"

"No, North Carolina."

"I thought you were a Virginian. You have a beautiful accent."

"Thank you."

"No corn pone or grits in it."

She laughed. "Well, what *do* you hear in my accent?"

"Quail, prime beef, and good whiskey."

"You must be hungry," she said.

"No, but I'm thirsty."

"Well, a bar has been set up over beneath those trees—over there? You see?"

"Come with me," I said.

"All right."

We walked over to the temporary bar where I got a bottle of cold beer and she a soft drink, and then we walked down a narrow, sun-and-shade-dappled path through the woods. There was a rich scent of vegetation there, resins and pollens, and it was quiet except for the birds and the whisper of wind in the treetops. She took my arm, although the path was not difficult.

"Why did you ask if I had been a cheerleader?" she asked.

"I had a vivid picture of you while we talked."

"What sort of picture?"

"In your tights and sweater."

"Oh, really? Well . . . "

"And then without your tights and sweater."

"Why, Mr. Racine, are you going to be lascivious now that you have me alone in the forest?"

"I had a picture of you on a Saturday afternoon in the late autumn. It's cold and clear, old men are burning leaves in the gutters, maple seeds are spinning down like tiny propellers. Everyone is going to the stadium for the game. Hip flasks and cold fried chicken in wicker baskets. And there you are on the sidelines, waving your big pom-poms."

She laughed.

"And you're smiling," I said. "In this picture, you're smiling and you have ninety-three perfect teeth."

"Mr. Racine, you surprise me."

"In what way?"

"Oh, the way you talk sometimes."

"I know. For twenty years, ever since I went into boxing on an amateur level, people have expressed surprise because I could pronounce words like 'sky' and 'tree' and 'night' without breaking them down into two or three syllables. I suppose it's my face, too."

"Why, there's nothing wrong with your face," she said. And then she laughed. "Although your nose is a *little* flat."

"I had a nearly aquiline nose before I came out of retirement a year ago."

"Aquiline?" She smiled.

"When I retired I had a cosmetic surgeon create a brand-new nose for me. It was a super nose, a three-thousand-dollar nose. Now he'll have to do it all over again."

We could hear the distance-muted hum of the big waterfall now. The path began to descend in tight switchbacks.

"I liked that nose," I said. "I used to stop and stare at its reflection in department-store windows."

She laughed. "You know, you aren't so gruff and surly when one gets to know you."

"I can be gruff and surly even to people who know me well. Shall we stop and have our drinks?"

"No, let's go on to the waterfall. It's so lovely there."

"And so," I said. "Where did you get your nose?"

"I was born with it."

"Where did you get your teeth?"

"I inherited them. An orthodontist helped, though."

"Where did you get your pom-poms?"

"They were issued to me when I was selected for the cheerleading team."

"You aren't so gruff and surly when one gets to know you," I said.

"My pom-poms seemed to have formed a bond between us, Mr. Racine."

We continued walking and then the forest gave way to a parklike area of grass and flowers. There were many bees, and I saw a hummingbird, an iridescent fluttering of light. Ahead we could see the long, foamy stream of the waterfall, curving in the wind gusts, throwing out smoky clouds of mist. A perfect rainbow arced through the mist.

We crossed a long field and sat on a wooden bench on the shore of the lake. The waterfall sounded like the roaring of great engines; we had to raise our voices to be understood.

"How in the world did you ever become a professional fighter?" she said.

"Long story."

"Are you in a hurry, Mr. Racine?"

"Call me Jim."

"Are you in a hurry, Jim?"

"Okay. When I was a kid I got into trouble with the police. A cop who liked kids got me to start coming around the Police Athletic League gym. You know, save a juvenile delinquent by taking the knife out of his hand and replacing it with a ball. It works in some cases. I played a little football, a little basketball, baseball, but what I really liked was boxing. I was an aggressive kid. I liked to hit people. I don't like to hit people anymore, I haven't liked it for years, but I liked it then."

The wind gusted and we were sprayed with a fine, cool mist.

"We should have gone to the other side of the lake," she said.

The wind diminished and we were again warmed by the sunlight.

"Well," she said. "Is that the end of the story?"

"I fought in the PAL program and then a little later I got into the AAU—that's the Amateur Athletic Union. I had talent. I did pretty well. Men who knew boxing helped me. One of the men got me an athletic scholarship to Stanford. I was good. The standard of boxing isn't all that high in college, and so I collected some trophies. I was a semifinalist in the Golden Gloves competition in 1964, and that got me selected to the U.S. Olympic boxing team. I was a substitute, I didn't get to fight, but they brought me along because with a little fasting or a little gluttony I could fight fairly well as either a light heavyweight or a heavyweight."

"And so then you became a professional?"

"No, then I got married and had a kid and got a job teaching P.E. in a Denver high school. I was assistant football coach; I wore a gray sweatshirt and hung a whistle around my neck. I told kids that sports would improve their character."

"Do they?"

"No, sports are just a source of pleasure, if they're approached right. That's not insignificant."

"No, I don't believe it would be."

"In my spare time I hung around the Denver gyms, sparred with the professionals, and one day a fight promoter asked me to fill a place on a card—one of the heavyweights had broken his hand. I told him no, I wasn't in shape. He offered me fifteen hundred dollars. I was making forty-eight hundred dollars a year at the time. I accepted. No one expected me to stay on my feet for more than three rounds. Hell, I was just a piece of meat they were throwing to a guy who was on his way up. He was a slugger, like the Caceras kid. Well, I cut him badly above his eye in the fourth round, and in the sixth round they stopped the fight. I had won. I was on my way."

"Have you done well?"

"Yes. I made a lot of money. I was ranked in the top ten for a time. I never had a really big payday, the kind the heavyweights are getting now, but I did okay."

"Then why did you come out of retirement last year?"

"There was a substantial divorce settlement. Substantial, hell—it was ruinous. And I had made a few bad investments, and then the tax people audited my returns . . . *Boxing* was the only way I knew how to make lot of money fast. I got in touch with Nacho—he's my manager now—and he set up this South American tour."

"But why didn't you fight in the States?"

"Because I'm too old. I'm not good enough anymore to get in the ring with any American heavyweight well known enough to make it a good payday. I wanted to make money, you see, but I didn't want to get hurt. But boxing is very popular down here, much more popular than in the States. People here like the sport, and they'll pay money to watch a fight between two good professionals. Ali doesn't have to be on the card to fill the stadium. And I still have a name down here, people remember that I was once the third-ranked heavyweight. In the States I'd be considered a desperate bum, another guy who lost his money and had to come back and be a punching bag."

Two boys were trying to skip flat stones across the water.

"Go on," she said.

"Nacho was able to get me some good paydays, and he put me in the ring against fighters that I could still handle. Except for Barboa, but that was just a three-round exhibition. And maybe except for Caceras, but Caceras had been hurt in his previous fight—he wasn't half himself."

"And so here we are," she said.

"Here we are."

"And have you made a lot of money on your tour?"

"Not a lot, but okay."

"What will you do now?"

"When I get out of this country? Well, a friend of mine, a former middleweight, has a small resort in Jamaica. A bar, a few cabañas, two sport-fishing boats. It's going to be a real money-maker, but he went a little too deeply in debt, and he's offered me a partnership. I think I'd like that. The tropical routine. Lots of sun, some deep-sea fishing and scuba diving with the guests, a white linen suit, cold gin and tonics in the bar at sunset. Sure, I could take that life."

"Well, I wish you luck," she said.

"Thank you. Your word with the ambassador might make a part of the luck unnecessary. Now, what about you? What is a nice Southern girl like you doing in the U.S. Foreign Service?"

"Oh, I'm afraid my life isn't as interesting as yours."

"My life hasn't been terribly interesting. A punch in the eye is definitely not interesting. Did you enter the Foreign Service directly out of college?"

"Yes. I spent a year in Washington, then two years in Rome, two in New Delhi, two back in Washington, and now here I am."

"You make it sound like lethargic tourism."

She smiled. "I've seen the Lincoln Memorial, the Vatican, the Taj Mahal, and now the Andes."

"Love?"

"One year in Washington, two years in Rome, two years in India—"

"And here? Now?"

She shrugged. "He's married?"

"The ambassador?"

"I've enjoyed our chat, Mr. Racine."

"It's been less a chat than a monologue," I said.

"What do you mean?"

"I don't usually tell my life story to a woman whom I've only recently met."

"Are you sorry now?"

"No. It may have been therapeutic. Will you have dinner with me some evening this week?"

"Why, yes, I will."

"Wednesday?"

"Fine. But I really must go now, I have so much to do. I'll talk to the ambassador this afternoon and arrange a little talk between you two."

"Good."

"How did you get here today?"

"A taxi. I sent it back to town."

"Well, if you'll meet us at the ambassador's limousine at six-thirty, you can ride back with us and talk to the ambassador then."

"That would be fine."

We both arose from the bench. She offered me her hand in a shy, oddly formal way, and then she smiled and started walking back toward the hotel complex. She was aware, of course, that I was watching her, and her walk was both self-conscious and provocative.

SEVEN

I did not want to miss my talk with the Ambassador, nor the ride back to the city, and so I walked over to the parking lot at six o'clock, a half hour early. The chauffeur was polishing a strip of the limousine's chrome. It looked as though he must have been waxing and polishing the big Cadillac all day; the chrome shone brilliantly in the angled late-afternoon sunlight, and I could clearly see my reflection in the glossy black door panel.

The chauffeur straightened and looked at me.

"I'll be riding back to the city with the ambassador," I said.

He nodded. "It will be crowded."

"I don't mind. Do you?"

He was a slender, black-haired young man in his late twenties. He was good-looking almost to the point of prettiness, with fine bones, a firm jawline, flat planes on his cheeks, a sensual mouth, and large, long-lashed brown eyes. He had removed his uniform jacket, but his tie was still tightly knotted at his throat, and he wore one of those absurd little caps with which chauffeurs are traditionally degraded. There was nothing servile about this man's eyes or attitude, though; he appeared self-assured to the point of arrogance.

"Sit in the car if you'd like," he said.

He had the slim, bold elegance of the ideal bullfighter, and like bullfighters he seemed concerned with holding *la línea.* "The line" was literal and aesthetic; your stance and carriage were very straight, shoulders back, head high, forcing the body to assume a graceful line. And *la línea* was also a vague philosophical concept; you kept your line, always, because it was an external manifestation of your inner pride and dignity, and no one and no thing should be capable of creating enough confusion or fear in you to make you lose your line. *Línea* means limit as well as line. You always appeared to be moving slowly; you never lost your serenity, your line, even in the most crucial situation.

He touched the hood of the car with his palm; a smeary print remained after he lifted his hand, began to fade, and then he wiped it away with a swipe of the cloth. He looked at me.

"You're Racine," he said. "The fighter." He spoke with only a trace of a Spanish accent.

"That's right," I said.

"I saw the fight."

I waited.

"I have seen Caceras fight eight, nine times. He looked very bad that night."

I nodded.

"The newspapers said something about drugs."

"The newspapers said a lot of things. Caceras wasn't drugged. He'd been hurt in another fight. He came back too soon."

"Who is responsible for that?"

I shrugged. "His manager, the medical board, himself."

"You didn't kill him, then?"

"Oh, yes, I killed him all right. But I had some help. Look, I figure that Caceras suffered some brain damage in his previous fight. Small hemorrhages in his brain, maybe—I don't know. But in some states in America a fighter has to take an electroencephalogram test before he's permitted to enter the ring. I don't think Caceras would have passed an EEG."

The chauffeur squinted off toward the sun. "Well," he said slowly. "I believe you would have beaten him at his best."

"Christ," I said. "You could probably get thrown in jail for saying something like that."

He smiled. "I'm a nationalist. But I'm not blind."

"Listen, have you been out here all day?"

He nodded. "Last week I left the car for a few minutes and some vandals damaged it. The ambassador gave me orders not to leave the vehicle when it was outside the embassy compound. He neglected to . . . "—he paused, searching for the right word—"rescind the order for today's picnic."

"Why didn't you ask permission?"

He gave me a look that clearly conveyed his feeling that a proud man didn't ask for anything.

"That's a hell of way to treat someone," I said.

"It isn't a matter of *treatment*," he said. "It's a matter of memory. If the ambassador had remembered his order, he would have rescinded it for today. This parking lot is guarded."

"Well, look, have you eaten?"

"The chauffeur from the Soviet Embassy brought me a bottle of beer and some corn."

"What time was that?"

"About noon."

"I'll be right back," I said.

I returned to the picnic area and filled a paper plate with slabs of beef and pork and a mound of potato salad; then I got two bottles of cold beer from one of the outdoor bars and returned to the car.

The chauffeur ate slowly, seriously, as if food were more an obligation than a pleasure, and then he wiped his hands on the car cloth and tasted his beer.

"Thank you," he said.

"You're welcome."

"What time does the ambassador plan to return to the city?" he asked.

"Six-thirty."

"These people are always late," he said. "They talk, they drink, they socialize." He said "these people" with great contempt; apparently he had decided that I was not one of "these people," that, in fact, I shared his feelings.

"You may have to wait here until nine or ten o'clock," he said.

I shrugged.

"I can arrange for you to get an earlier ride to the city. I have friends who will be leaving soon."

"I have business with the ambassador," I said.

He nodded. "Well, then . . . Shall we listen to the radio?"

The ambassador and his group arrived at seven-twenty. There was the ambassador, Gordon Fox; Alicia Phillips; Dan Grogan, the assistant commercial attaché and/or CIA chief of station; and two other men, both tall, lean, with short hair and a military bearing. I heard the ambassador call one of the men "Major." Perhaps, then, he was the military attaché or a member of the Marine detachment assigned to security duty at the embassy.

"Fine picnic, wasn't it, Raoul?" Ambassador Fox asked the chauffeur.

"Very nice, sir. Much better than last year's picnic," the chauffeur said as he placed the two heavy golf bags in the trunk.

"Raoul, put on your jacket, do you mind? It's unprofessional for you to be in your shirtsleeves."

"Yes sir. I'm sorry, Ambassador." Raoul was smiling faintly; the tone of his voice was insolent. He held his line.

"I know it's hot," the ambassador said. "Still, there's a certain dignified image we must maintain."

The ambassador was wearing a white fishnet shirt, chocolate-brown slacks, and brown and white spiked golf shoes.

Alicia Phillips introduced me to the four men: Ambassador Fox, Dan Grogan, Major Brecht, and Captain Datone. The military men were formally polite; Grogan, friendly and casual and perhaps a little patronizing; and the ambassador had pretended that my grip had hurt his hand—he went into a crouch, moaning, and then he quickly straightened and feinted twice with his left hand.

The ambassador was about my height and weight, but oddly proportioned, heavy through the waist and buttocks, with a narrow chest and coat-hanger shoulders and a curiously long, thin neck, which looked much too fragile to support his massive head. His face was squarish, tanned, handsome in a whiskey-advertisement sort of way. He was about fifty years old; younger-looking in the face, older-looking in the body. I could smell alcohol on his breath; he was just a couple more drinks away from being sloppy, fall-down drunk.

Raoul closed the trunk lid, got his jacket from the front seat, put it on, and then walked around, opening doors for us. Grogan and Major Brecht sat in the front, next to the chauffeur; Captain Datone sat by the left-hand rear door; the ambassador was in the center, and then Alicia Phillips. I sat on the fold-out jump seat.

"Four, three, two, one . . . launch!" the ambassador said.

Raoul drove slowly out of the parking lot, paused at the ALTO sign, then turned toward the city.

I looked at Alicia Phillips. She returned my gaze and smiled briefly, the kind of automatic smile you receive from store clerks after you've bought something expensive, and then turned and looked out the window.

"Jack, why don't you mix some toddies for us?" the ambassador said. *"Escocés y agua* for me."

There was a compact little bar built into a drawer that slid out from the rear of the forward seat; inside were bottles of Scotch, bourbon, and rum, along with water, tonic, fruit, and a compartment of ice. The ice was mostly melt-water now. Captain Datone made a weak Scotch and water for the ambassador.

"Thanks, Jack. What will you have, Jim?"

"Nothing, sir," I said.

"Are you in training?"

"Yes." It was always easy to refuse a drink if you were a boxer.

He sipped his drink. "Christ, Jack, there isn't any *escocés* in this *escocés y agua."*

"You have to attend the reception at the Mexican Embassy this evening," Alicia Phillips said coolly. I got the impression that she was angry at Fox.

"Damn!" the ambassador said. "What a fine day! What do you think, Charlie?"

"Wonderful," Major Brecht said in the front seat.

"Charlie, you told me about bringing my hands through behind the club head and it cost you a few bucks, didn't it? You bet. Better than last year's picnic, right, Raoul?"

"Yes sir."

"A great day. But tonight I have to go to one of those guacamole receptions in honor of—what the hell is his name, Alicia?"

"Anselmo Moya."

"There, you see? Who the hell is Anselmo Moya? Sometimes I wonder why I accepted this lousy job."

He had not accepted the lousy job, he'd bought it with a huge campaign contribution. My source at the embassy was contemptuous of Ambassador Fox, not only because he was not a career diplomat, but also because Quitasol was considered a poor assignment— "Christ, anyone who bled that much money into a presidential campaign should have been posted to London or Paris or Rome. Quitasol—you should be able to buy the ambassadorship here for peanuts. But Fox is an ass— not even *that* administration was cynical enough to send him anywhere important." Fox, my source said, had become a multimillionaire through the invention and marketing of a glue useful in the lamination of fiberglass. Not his invention—"The son of a bitch stole the rights and royalties from a chemist who worked for him."

Grogan half turned and glanced at us one by one. He seemed amused and expectant, as if the performance in the back seat were bound to improve.

"Jack," he said, "would you mix me a Scotch and water too? And remember that I don't have to attend any receptions tonight."

He looked at me. He was a green-eyed redhead, and his stare was very direct. "I saw you whip Caceras," he said.

I did not speak.

"Did you ever kill a man before?"

"Dan!" Alicia Phillips said. "For God's sake!"

"Did you?"

"No," I said. "Have you?"

He smiled and nodded. Captain Datone handed him his drink and he turned to look ahead through the windshield. "Yes," he said. "But never with my hands."

"Dan . . . " Alicia Phillips said in a low tone.

Grogan turned to look at me. "I hit a kid with my car when I was seventeen," Grogan said. "She became as dead as Caceras, and it took just about as long. We have something in common."

"I don't think we do," I said.

"The Equator is coming up," Ambassador Fox said. "Would you stop the car there, Raoul? I've always wanted to stand with one foot in the Northern Hemisphere and one in the Southern."

The chauffeur gradually slowed the car and then pulled off onto the gravel alongside the road. There was a stone obelisk with a greenish-colored copper plate which announced that the famous Equator crossed this spot. A yellow stripe crossed the highway here, and so the geographical abstraction of the Equator became, for thirty feet, an actual line.

Captain Datone got out of the car and held the door open for the ambassador.

"Anyone else?" the ambassador said.

No one responded.

"There is no romance in your souls!" he cried. He got out of the car, walked to the center of the road, and straddled the line.

"The hell with you!" he cried. "I'm astride the Equator!" And then, laughing, he returned to the car. "Jesus," he said. "It started out to be fun, and I learned that it was magic."

The chauffeur waited for two cars to pass and then he eased the limousine back out into the highway. We crossed the yellow stripe and for an instant my legs were in the Northern Hemisphere while the rest of my body remained behind in the Southern. It was not an especially exciting moment.

"Mr. Ambassador," I said. "I hope you'll be able to help me. There is really no reason I should be forced to remain in this country."

"What? Oh, yes, Alicia told me about your predicament. Don't worry about a thing, Jim, I'll have it fixed by noon tomorrow."

"Thank you."

"I'll simply express a bit of curiosity in your position and those fellows will get the point. I'll build a small fire and see who fries."

"Thank you," I said again, but I was thinking that he was a lazy son of a bitch if the expression of a little curiosity was all that was required to free an illegally detained American citizen and he had not had the time or interest to employ it.

The chauffeur began slowing the car.

"Raoul, hit the goddamned gas, son. I've got to

take a nap and shower and shave and what all for that reception."

"There's something wrong with the car," Raoul said. "The carburetion, I think . . . "

I could see Raoul's eyes in the rear-view mirror. I looked out the back window and saw a car about two hundred yards behind us. It gained rapidly and then swung out to pass. The occupants waved—picnic guests apparently, on their way back to the city.

"Christ, can't you make this thing go any faster?"

"It isn't the carburetion," the major said. "The engine sounds like it's running smoothly enough."

"There's just no power," Raoul said.

I saw his eyes in the rear-view mirror again. I turned and looked back; the road was empty. The car ahead of us was far away now, and then it vanished around a corner.

The car slowed a little and then Raoul twisted the wheel and we turned off onto a dirt road that climbed through scrub brush and cactus country.

"Where the hell are you *going?*" the ambassador said.

"I think the car is going to stop running," Raoul said. His face was glossy with a sheen of sweat, and his eyes, in the rear-view mirror, were very large and rounded; I could see white all the way around his pupils.

"Stop the car!" the ambassador ordered.

"I know a good mechanic . . . just a little farther . . . around that curve ahead . . . a very good mechanic."

Captain Datone hurriedly opened a small box built into the door and removed a .45 caliber pistol.

"Oh, shit," Major Brecht said. "I left my pistol in the golf bag."

"Now just what the hell is going on?" Ambassador Fox said. "There aren't any mechanics out in this God-forsaken country."

Captain Datone worked the pistol's slide, bringing a cartridge up out of the clip and into the chamber. The hammer was back. He pressed the muzzle against the back of Raoul's head.

"Stop the car right now," he said coldly.

"How could I have been so stupid!" the major said in anguish, referring to having left his gun in the golf bag.

Dan Grogan was slowly shaking his head. Alicia Phillips had covered her mouth with the fingers of her right hand. The ambassador was frowning.

"Stop the car, Raoul!" Captain Datone said.

"Soon," Raoul said. "Just over this hill . . . a friend of mine . . . a very good mechanic . . . "

Captain Datone pulled the trigger, and the hammer fell with a click. He quickly worked the slide again, pressed the pistol against Raoul's head, and pulled the trigger. Another click.

"The son of a bitch filed off the firing pin!" the captain said.

And then we were around the curve and dropping down a hill. An old Ford truck blocked the road. There was a yellow Volkswagen behind it. Raoul pressed the horn button, and at the sound some men rose up from the ditches alongside the road. They wore ordinary civilian clothes and they were all armed.

Raoul stopped the car, opened the door, and was part-way out when Captain Datone swung his pistol. The blow struck Raoul on his left cheek, and then he was out on the ground, rolling over and over toward the ditch.

The ambassador was very pale. "I have diplomatic immunity," he said softly.

Grogan grinned. "Foxy," he said, "I get the impression that those folks are not going to recognize your immunity."

"*Fuera!*" one of the men shouted, waving his machine pistol. "*Fuera!*" Get out!

"Well," Grogan said. "I don't think they'll let us sulk here for very long. Let's go."

EIGHT

We lined up with our backs against the limousine. They looked us over.

The sun had fallen behind the western sierra, but the clouds still burned with incandescent orange and crimson and peach colors. Dusk was swiftly approaching from the east, gliding down the slopes of the volcanoes, carrying a new night smell and coolness.

There were seven of them: Raoul, who had thrown away his chauffeur's cap and jacket and now carried a revolver; a slender, crazy-eyed girl who looked very much like Raoul, perhaps his sister; two Indians who wore their crow-black hair in bangs; a tall black man whose head had been shaved; another girl, who did not appear to be more than fifteen years old; and a short, powerfully built man who was nearly as broad as he was tall.

Raoul's cheek was bleeding. He did not seem to notice; he paced back and forth in front of us, looking happy. I did not know which to fear most; his happiness or the others' quiet seriousness.

"*Bien hecho,*" Raoul said. Well done.

"The embassy chauffeur," Grogan said softly. "My God, that's security . . . "

Raoul grinned. He stood very straight, holding *la línea*. "I wasn't a revolutionary when I was hired," he said. "You fools helped to convert me."

"You people aren't revolutionaries or guerrillas," the ambassador said scornfully.

"Shut up," Major Brecht said.

"No, I won't shut up. I'm not afraid of this mercenary scum. Bandits!"

"*Él,*" Raoul said, pointing his revolver at the ambassador. "*Él.*" (Dan Grogan). "*Y ella.*" (Alicia Phillips). Those three were dragged away from the car and forced to lie prone on the dusty road.

Major Brecht, to my left, was breathing very rapidly, hyperventilating. He bent at the knees and then, with an effort, straightened. Captain Datone was trying to smile, but it was the fragmented smile of a small child, one that could go either way, into laughing or weeping. I repeatedly licked my lips, but there was no moisture on my swollen tongue. There were many important things I wanted to say, but my mouth was too dry and my tongue too thick to mold my thoughts into words. And my vision was affected; my peripheral vision was clear, but whatever I stared at directly was blurry, misted.

The stocky man did not step forward, his companions moved away, and he was isolated before us. He had a black beard. His eyes reminded me of chips of coal, totally black but still capable of reflecting light. He lifted his machine pistol.

"Wait," Raoul said. He gestured with his revolver. "Racine, go over there with the others. That plate of food saved your life, my friend."

I walked away from the limousine, away from Brecht and Datone, toward life. My legs were stiff, numb; it was as if I had borrowed another man's legs for those fifteen paces. I felt insulated from myself; this was not me, this dull entity was only a dream fragment of myself.

The machine pistol stuttered. I could hear the sound of bullets striking flesh and the almost simultaneous clanking noise as they struck the car behind. I turned. Major Brecht was sprawled out in the dust. The back of his shirt was spotted with blood. There were silver-rimmed holes in the door of the limousine. Captain Datone was crying soundlessly. His eyes were closed; tears wet his cheeks; his lips writhed. His legs were trembling and he held his arms out, palms up, as if presenting a gift. The machine pistol rattled, his body slammed back against the car, delicate flowers of blood blooming on his shirt, and then he pitched forward into the road.

Alicia had closed her eyes. The ambassador, lying prone, said over and over again, "Oh, my God! Oh, my God! Oh, my God!" Dan Grogan breathed fast and deeply; tiny puffs of dust erupted with each exhalation.

I was numb, still dreaming. But I thought, vaguely, about how trivial the barrier can be between life and death; a few slices of beef and pork on a paper plate. A simple gesture which could not even be characterized as kindness. Two dollars worth of food. My life was worth two dollars. At that instant I ceased regarding my life as an objective fact—it was really a sort of whimsical notion of possibilities. I was not alive and I was not dead. But I could now imagine the possibility of either.

PART TWO
UNDERGROUND

NINE

We were searched and then the black man, the two Indians, and the very young girl were taken aside to receive their instructions. They listened intently, nodding, and then they got into the Volkswagen and drove around the truck and down the dirt road toward the highway. Raoul, the girl who resembled him, and the thickset bearded man, whom Raoul called "Oso," remained with us.

Oso and the girl climbed into the back of the truck.

"Get up off the ground, Ambassador," Raoul said. He had stuck the revolver in his belt. Oso was covering us with his machine pistol from the back of the truck.

"Please, Raoul," the ambassador said. "Why are you doing this to us?"

"Get up," Raoul said. "Sir."

The ambassador slowly rose to his feet. His face was dust-and-sweat-streaked and his lower lip was bleeding—perhaps he had bitten it. He looked absurd in his golfing clothes.

"Get into the back of the truck," Raoul said.

We waited a couple of minutes and then Alicia was ordered to go to the truck. She was very pale and her eyes were dilated. She had lost a shoe somewhere but she did not pause to look for it. She moved slowly, almost languidly, as if she had just been awakened.

"Grogan," Raoul said.

Grogan's kinky red hair was powdered with yellow dust. He was smiling and he moved naturally. I admired him for that.

Everything seemed to be taking a long time, but I estimated that we had not been here more than fifteen minutes. The colors were just beginning to fade from the sky.

"All right," Raoul said to me.

I did not want them to mistake my intentions—they seemed more wary of me than the others, probably because I was a professional fighter—and so I placed my hands behind my head and was careful to move slowly.

"That's a good boy," Raoul said, grinning."

I had to use my hands to clamber into the back of the truck. Oso was forward in the shadows. The ambassador, Grogan, and Alicia were sitting on a wooden bench that ran the length of the truck bed, and their right arms were raised in what looked like a limp-wristed fascist salute; but then I saw that their wrists had been tied with rawhide thongs to the steel roll bar overhead.

"Sit down," the girl said.

I sat on the end of the bench and raised my right hand. The girl stepped forward and tied one end of a

rawhide strip tightly around my wrist and the other end
to the roll bar.

Grogan was sitting next to me. He smelled of sweat
and dust.

The girl buckled the canvas end flaps closed and
then it was dark except for little blurs of yellowish light
overhead where the canvas had worn thin. The girl
switched on a flashlight and directed the beam on our
wrists while Oso examined the knots. Then they both
sat down on the wooden bench opposite us.

Oso's black eyes gleamed moistly in the general
glow of the flashlight. His nose was a hooked beak that
started straight and then abruptly bent down and to one
side. Silver hair glinted in his thick black beard. Oso—
Bear—was a good name for him; he was built like a
bear, looked like one, and seemed to possess the ursine's
grave, ponderous stupidity.

The girl was pretty despite her facial rigidity (perhaps
caused by fear) and the hot intensity of her stare. Without
those, and with a little attention to grooming and clothes,
she might have been beautiful. But beauty is anti-revolu-
tionary, gaiety is bourgeois, and individuality must always
be subordinated to the capital-C Cause. The personal ego
loses itself in the collective Movement Ego. This country
and a great many others needed a Revolution, maybe all
countries do, but they could get along very well without
the revolutionaries. I looked into the girl's hot smoky eyes
and thought that she was probably crazy. She returned
my stare sullenly for a moment and then suddenly locked
her teeth together in a ferocious grin.

Raoul, up in the cab now, started the engine. I heard the dry clanking of gears and then we started moving. The girl turned off her flashlight and it was dark beneath the canopy. The truck moved forward and back, forward and back again, turning around, and then we were moving down the dirt road toward the highway. I could smell exhaust fumes. The truck was in bad shape: the shocks and springs were loose, the engine was missing, the transmission gears engaged with a grinding shudder—these people had taken a hell of a chance to kidnap the American ambassador in a vehicle that might break down at any moment. What would they do then, hitchhike?

It was a smoother ride when we turned off onto the highway. We turned left, south. I could hear the humming of the tires on the pavement.

Oso struck a match and his face was briefly illuminated as he leaned over it to light a cigarette. The match went out and it was dark again except for the glowing and dimming of the cigarette coal as he smoked.

We were on the highway for about twenty minutes and then we turned off onto a bumpy, rutted side road. That road ran straight for five minutes and then I could feel the centrifugal force as we made a sweeping turn to the left, another to the right, and the road became a series of uniform curves which gradually reduced in radius until we were moving up a steep incline in hairpin turns. I could feel the cant of the truck. The engine whined in low gear. The road deteriorated; I would have been thrown from the bench several times if I hadn't been tied to the roll bar. My wrist hurt; my fingers were numbing. The air was cool now and it began to smell like iron.

Oso lit another cigarette.

"Could I have a cigarette?" Grogan said loudly. He had to nearly shout to be heard above the stuttering engine and the persistent whine of the gearbox.

"He doesn't know English," the girl said.

Across from us the orange cigarette coal glowed and dimmed, glowed and dimmed, and was then stamped into sparks on the floorboards.

The truck continued grinding up the mountainside. We were very high now; it was cool, the air was no longer scented with vegetation, and I could feel the early effects of oxygen deprivation.

"Won't even give me a cigarette," Grogan said. "What a shabby bunch of terrorists."

"Shut up," the girl said.

"No class," Grogan said, and then he was silent.

The truck went on for another ten minutes and then stopped. Raoul raced the engine to fill the carburetor with gas, and at the peak of rpm's switched off the ignition. The engine softly popped and creaked. I could smell hot metal and hot exhaust fumes. Wind, entering beneath the rear flaps, ballooned the canvas hood.

"Bring them out one at a time," Raoul called.

Oso held the flashlight in his left hand, the machine pistol in his right, while the girl released the ambassador from the overhead bar; then she took the loose end of rawhide and tied his hands before him. She expertly whipped the rawhide around his wrists and tied a knot, two more loops, and then another knot. Women are rarely so adept at knot-tying; I assumed that she had practiced.

The canvas flaps were unbuckled and the Ambassador clumsily dismounted from the platform. Alicia was next; then Grogan; and then me.

We were high on one of the volcanoes. I could see the lights of a village far below; and above, shining cold and hard, the crystalline glitter of unfamiliar constellations. The moon illuminated a landscape similar to its own: ash-colored soil, stones, rocks, huge rectangular-cut black boulders, shadows like spilled ink, desolation. A cold wind blew down off the glacier. And we could see the glacier, foreshortened from this angle, shining like a shadowed, wind-rippled lake in the moonlight.

We split into two groups and started up the twisting footpath. Raoul and the girl went ahead, guarding the ambassador and Alicia Phillips; Grogan followed about fifty feet behind them. I trailed Grogan, and Oso and his machine pistol was at the end of the snaking line.

It was quite cold now; the wind, smelling of ice, gusted down the mountainside with a sound like a fast river. The path, the surrounding terrain, was familiar to me: This was the path that led up to the old man's cave. We were at about fourteen thousand feet here. The cave was another thousand vertical feet higher; the summit of the volcano close to five thousand feet higher than that.

We moved very slowly, pausing often to rest. I was the only one who was not severely affected by the altitude.

The others coughed dryly, stumbled, complained of headaches and nausea.

It took us three hours to reach the cave. I had walked the same distance in less than an hour a few days ago. I was the only one in the group who was in good physical condition. That might mean something.

TEN

Candles were burning inside the cave and their light was reflected in the rock's thousand facets, winking blurs—it was like being imprisoned in the center of a great dark crystal. The cave smelled of incompletely tanned goatskins and burning animal fats. The old man was there. I do not think he recognized me. He looked frightened, bewildered by what was happening in his cave, his life.

I was ordered to pick up one of the tallow candles and go through the passageway at the rear of the cave. I moved down the narrow rock corridor for about thirty feet and then there was a sharp-angled turn to the left. I had to duck my head now, and my shoulders brushed against the rock.

It was cool, musty-smelling, and the walls were wet with condensation. Our footsteps echoed dully. The passageway turned again and began to descend. There were primitive, stylized drawings chiseled out of the black rock walls—pre-Columbian graffiti?—but I could only glance at them in passing. I squeezed side-

ways through a narrow slit in the rock and abruptly
entered a huge, high-ceilinged chamber. At first I sensed
the increase in space rather than saw it: the silence
itself had a different, humming quality, and the various
noises—water dripping somewhere, the scrape of our
shoes on rock, Raoul's command, *"Andale!"*—traveled
farther to reach their limits and return to our ears. I
knew the room was large by a kind of primitive human
radar. Alicia Phillips came up and stood beside me. She
was carrying a candle, too. The powerful bearded man,
Oso, carried a long four-cell flashlight. But the dimen-
sions of the room were defined as much by shadow
as light. It was about the size of a gymnasium, with
a domed ceiling and water-smoothed walls. The floor
was littered with slabs and blocks of stone which had
fallen from the ceiling, and in the quivering merger of
light and shadow they looked like avant-garde furniture for a race of giants.

The ambassador, Grogan, Alicia, and I were ordered
to move forward, into the center of the cave.

"Put down the candles," Raoul said. His voice was
deepened and amplified by the cave.

I placed my candle on the stone floor; Alicia hesitated and then did the same.

"Sara, *las lumínicas,*" Raoul said.

We waited. The girl materialized out of the shadows and circled behind us. She cut the rawhide thongs
tying our hands, then picked up the candles and
walked away. Our light was gone now, but its borders
remained in our minds: we would remain in this place,

at least for a time, like dogs who had been unclipped from their chains and yet are afraid to venture beyond the old safe perimeter.

"I'll kill any of you who leave this chamber," Raoul said.

And then the lights receded, dimmed, vanished.

We were immersed in total darkness. This was blackness beyond the concept of blackness; no grays, no pinpoints of starlight, nothing. It was not a darkness like mere night: this was thicker, heavier, and seemed to exert a pressure similar to the pressure you feel when diving in deep water. The floor, walls, and ceiling became a vise in our minds.

"Don't anyone panic," Ambassador Fox said, panic vibrating in his voice.

Alicia, next to me, was breathing very rapidly.

"Don't be frightened," the ambassador said.

"Look," Grogan said, "let's all join hands in a circle, sit down and talk things out." His voice, heard through the cave's humming resonance and dull echoes, sounded normal.

"Yes, yes," Fox said. "Yes, now we'll link hands and discuss this situation."

I thought it was foolish, but the others seemed to need the human contact and so I went along with them. We joined hands in a line, me to Alicia, she to Grogan, Grogan to the ambassador, and then the line curved and the ambassador and I groped in the darkness, found each other's hand, and closed the circle. We slowly lowered ourselves down to the cold stone floor.

"Are you okay, Alicia?" Grogan asked.

"Yes," she said, but she did not sound okay; her voice was high, almost shrill, and her breathing remained unnaturally fast.

"Let's try to figure the angles," Grogan said.

"I'll tell you the angle," Fox said. "This is an attempt to humiliate the government of the United States of America." His hand was surprisingly small, and it was warm and moist with sweat.

"They want money," Grogan said.

It was quiet then. The walls seemed to glide in closer during the silences; our voices temporarily pushed them back again.

"I know this country," I said.

They listened.

"I've been here before. I met the old man last week. I was hiking and he invited me into the outer cave for lunch. I know the way down."

They remained silent.

"If the four of us—you too, Alicia, you'll have to help—if all of us jump them tonight . . . "

"No," the ambassador said, alarmed. "They'll kill us!"

"There are just three of them out there."

"Four," Grogan said.

"I don't think the old man is involved in this. Anyway, he's old and fragile—Alicia could distract him."

"You're talking crap!" Fox said, quietly furious. He removed his hand from mine.

"Just three we have to worry about. Raoul, the girl, and Oso. I don't know where the other four went, but we can assume that they'll come here sooner or later. We won't have a chance then. But now . . . "

"You'll get us all killed, man!" Fox said.

"They might kill us anyway," I said. "Look, they'll probably leave a sentry to guard the entrance to the tunnel and then the others will sleep."

"I'll have nothing to do with it," the ambassador said. "Grogan?"

He was quiet for a time and then he said, "No. The tunnel mouth is too narrow, we'd have to come out one at a time. A man with an automatic rifle . . . No, they've got us, Racine."

"I'll go through first."

"No, Racine. Not now. I don't think they intend to hurt us."

I said, "Do you think they'll free us if they get their ransom money?"

"Yes, I think so."

"Why did they kill Brecht and Datone?"

"Because they weren't of any use."

Silence, and then the ambassador asked, "Of what use is *he?*"

It was a valid question, but I didn't like the phrasing.

"Raoul didn't kill me because I brought him a plate of food this afternoon," I said.

"What?" Fox, incredulous.

"That's right."

"I can't believe that. A plate of food?"

"You left him in the parking lot all day. In the sun and heat. I gave him a plate of food and a bottle of beer."

"And you expect us to believe that those blood-thirsty rats would spare your life out of *gratitude?*"

"I don't care whether you believe it or not," I said.

"And you said that you know these people."

"I didn't say I knew those people, I said I knew the country and that I had met the old man."

They were silent.

"Oh, for Christ's sake!" I said.

"Well," Grogan said quietly. "It is a coincidence."

"Sure," I said. "I'm one of them. So is Alicia—she invited me to ride back in the limousine this afternoon. This kidnapping is the reason why I'm in this miserable country. The Caceras fight is just cover. Is that the right word, Grogan? Cover. And tell me, Grogan, why didn't they kill you along with Brecht and Datone?"

"They want information from me, not dollars," Grogan said.

"Are you really with the CIA?"

"Yes."

"Okay, baby," I said to Alicia. "Justify the fact that you're breathing."

"Leave her alone," Fox said.

I squeezed her hand. "Are you rich?"

"No."

"Is your family rich?"

"No."

"You must be a secret agent. How much money could your family raise if they had to?"

"I don't *know.*"

"Racine, this isn't getting us anywhere," Grogan said.

"Guess," I said to her.

"I just don't know!"

"One hundred thousand dollars?"

"I suppose so. Yes."

"Two hundred thousand dollars?"

"I don't know. Perhaps."

"Three hundred thousand dollars?"

"I don't know."

"All right. You're an employee of the U.S. Embassy and your family doesn't eat dog food on weeknights. You've earned the right to breathe."

"Cool off, Racine," Grogan said.

"Is Raoul working for the Russians?" I asked.

"No," Grogan said.

"The Cubans? The Chinese?"

"No. If Raoul were working for *any* intelligence organization, his masters would want him to remain right where he was. Chauffeur at the U.S. Embassy? That would be a valuable position. No, these people are on their own."

"What are their politics, do you think?"

"I don't know. Probably they're Marxist nationalists. Most of these terrorist groups are."

"Could they be right-wing terrorists?"

"No," Grogan said. "All of the right-wing terrorists are already employed by the government."

"The filthy scum," Ambassador Fox said.

"They're amateurs," Grogan said.

"How do you know?" I asked.

"They were all very nervous except for the animal who did the killing. Raoul was scared too, but he controlled his fear. The others just stood around. They seemed confused, just as frightened as we were. None of them went down the road to prevent any cars from approaching—bad planning or someone missed an assignment. And the girl and one of the Indians got sick after the murders."

"You observed more than I did."

"I don't think they've been in business long. This was probably their first operation. They were not well armed; one machine pistol, a couple of old rifles, handguns, a double-barreled shotgun . . . But they were smart enough to wear civilian clothes. A lot of these little paramilitary outfits are romantics, playing at being soldiers, and usually the first thing they do is put on army fatigues and assign rank—Latin America has more self-appointed generals and colonels than you can count. But uniforms are stupid unless you have a force big enough to engage in regular military battles."

"Dan," the ambassador said, "you talk as if that rabble was some sort of military organization."

"Well, you never know. Castro started with just a few men and look at him now."

"Filth," the ambassador said. "Terrorists."

"I'm terrified," Grogan said.

"What is going to happen to us?" Alicia asked.

"I don't know. We'll just have to wait and see."

"We might have to wait for months," I said.

"The State Department will ransom me," Fox said. "Me," he said, not "us."

"No they won't," Grogan said. "But maybe your family will."

"I guess there's nothing more to discuss," I said. "Either we attempt to escape or wait to be ransomed. That might take three weeks, two months, forever." I removed my hand from Alicia's.

"Where are you going?" she asked.

"I'm going to practice waiting."

I made myself as comfortable as I possibly could on the uneven rock floor. My eyes were open but I could see nothing but glowing retinal specks. This darkness was an intimation of death's long night. Darkness and silence. The silence itself was a sound; it hummed and faintly crackled, like the "sound of the sea" in a conch shell, except that it was greatly amplified in this chamber—this silence was like the remote roaring of a waterfall.

I thought of the rainbow-streaked waterfall at Vistahermosa. I pictured it as it poured whitely down the cliffside, wind-curved, smoking mist, and then thundering down into the lake. I imagined myself lying flat on the wet grass and drinking deeply from the lake. The water was so cold that my throat and teeth ached. I was thirsty. Hunger waited behind the thirst. And I was tired. The body continues making its incessant demands no matter what the circumstances. Tomorrow I might be dead; tonight I was thirsty, hungry, and fatigued.

Alicia began weeping softly, privately. The humming cave echoed her sobs, increased them; it sounded like a score of ghostly crying women. The echoes sounded sympathetic at first, and then they seemed to become mocking.

And then I was asleep. I dreamed of the murders of Major Brecht and Captain Datone; they died over and over again. I was helpless. Not even my devious, clever dream-mind could act to save them.

ELEVEN

I awakened. Cold, humming darkness, voices.

I sat up. "What is it?"

"All hell has broken loose out there, Racine." Grogan's voice.

"Out where?"

"In the outer cave."

"What is this all about, Grogan?"

"They captured some of them," Alicia said. "How many, Dan? Three of them?"

"Grogan," I said, "what's happening?"

"They'll get what they damn well deserve now," the ambassador said. "The vicious punks!"

"I don't know what you people are talking about."

"Okay, listen," Grogan said. "I crawled part way down the tunnel a few hours ago, down to the first bend. I wanted to see if I could hear what their plans were, or if we could rush them, as you suggested, Racine. It was quiet. They were probably all sleeping except for a guard. But then about twenty minutes ago someone came in from the outside. One of the Indians, I think—they called him Tono. He woke them up. The kid was nearly hysterical, and the others got excited too, and I had a hell of a time piecing it together. But the police have captured three of the four who left in the Volkswagen. They were supposed to return to their homes in the city, go back to their jobs, and they dropped off the Indian boy—Tono— and then afterwards the car got stopped in a roadblock. The cops found guns in the car. The Indian kid came up here to warn the others."

"This may not be good for us, Grogan," I said.

"I know."

"What do you mean, 'not good'?" the ambassador said. "This is the best thing that could have happened."

"No, it's all blown up in their faces," Grogan said. "They might decide to kill all of us now."

"What? No! What did you say?"

I said, "Did you hear anything else, Grogan?"

"Raoul kept repeating, 'Twenty-four hours, they promised us twenty-four hours.'"

"What do you think that means?"

"I don't know, but I'd guess that all of them had previously agreed that if they were captured and tortured they'd try to hold out for twenty-four hours."

"Anything else?"

"No. I was afraid that they'd start down the tunnel after us. I got away from there."

"They won't hurt us, will they, Dan?" Alicia asked.

He was quiet for a moment. "I don't know."

"They'll release us now," the ambassador said firmly.

"Who is out there now?" I asked Grogan.

"Raoul, the girl, Oso, the Indian boy, and the old man."

"The police will be here in three hours," the ambassador said confidently.

"Look, Grogan," I said. "We've got to take a chance and jump them when they come for us."

"Right. We'll jump them when they come out of the tunnel."

"I'll have nothing to do with this," Fox said.

"Let's go, Grogan," I said, and I stood up, but it was too late: we heard sounds at the tunnel entrance and then a bright cone of light leaped across the darkness and shined on us. I was blinded by the light.

"Racine." Raoul's voice.

"What?" I said, shielding my eyes.

"Come with us."

"Why?"

"We're freeing you."

"Get the light out of my eyes."

The beam was lowered, and after a moment I could see the black stone floor of the cave, the slabs and blocks of rubble, and nearby, looking up at me, Grogan and Fox and Alicia. Their faces were very pale in the light; the colors of their clothing were a surprise—I had forgotten about color.

"Come on now, Racine," Raoul said. "You aren't involved in this, we're letting you go."

I started moving slowly toward the light.

"Sorry, Racine," Grogan said quietly.

"Yeah."

"Look them right square in their fucking eyes," he said.

"What are they going to do?" Fox asked.

"Shut up," Grogan said.

"They won't hurt him. He's one of them."

"Just shut up," Grogan said.

Raoul and Oso followed me down the twisting tunnel. I knew that I was going to die. I knew it but I couldn't wholly believe it. I saw a vivid picture of Captain Datone as he died. He had held out his hands as if to bribe them with a gift; but now I realized that what he'd held in his cupped hands was not any sort of gift, it was his life and he was showing it to them, wordlessly saying, Look, see how beautiful it is, how perfect and unique, this is the one thing that no man has a right to steal from another. And they'd shot him. Had Captain Datone believed that they could refuse so eloquent an appeal? What could I do or say that would stop them?

False dawn filled the small outer cave with a transparent milky light. The girl, sitting on a wooden crate, looked up at me; there was no shame or pity in her eyes. The old man turned away from my glance. The Indian, holding a double-barreled shotgun, stood just outside the cave entrance.

"Keep walking," Raoul said. His voice was very low and soothing.

We passed through the cave opening and began descending the steep talus slope. The Indian covered me with his shotgun from the side while Raoul and Oso followed me. The valley far below was covered by a layer of cauliflowered clouds. It was very cold; my breath smoked, and I could smell the glacier above us, and the ironlike odor of the rocks. The thin air had a slightly bitter taste.

"Stop there," Raoul said.

I turned.

The Indian, still guarding me with his shotgun, backed uphill a few yards, then turned and started climbing back toward the cave. Raoul and Oso were standing about thirty feet above me on the slope. Oso had his machine pistol; Raoul was unarmed. The Indian climbed past them. Beyond the Indian I could see the girl standing in the entrance arch, looking down upon us; above her, foreshortened by perspective, were the glacier and the summit, and beyond the summit nothing but sky.

"I'm sorry, Racine," Raoul said. He really sounded sorry, more than a little sad. "The situation has changed."

"Wait!" I said. I cleared my throat. "Wait, give me just one minute. You owe me a minute."

"It's best to get it over with," he said sadly.

"One minute, Raoul, for Christ's sake!"

He shrugged "Okay."

"You're going to have to get away, out of the country, or you're going to have to hide. I have money. I'll trade you the money for my life."

"How much money do you have?"

"More than thirteen thousand dollars in this country."

"Where is it?"

"In a savings account in a Quitasol bank."

"And you think that you can just walk into the bank and withdraw your money?"

"Why not? Sure I can."

"Because you were kidnapped yesterday," he said dryly.

"Who knows that?"

"*Mata lo,*" Oso said. Kill "it," not *him.*

"Raoul, Jesus, man, listen. I just happened to be in the limousine by accident. You know that. No one *knows* I was with the ambassador. I just happened to get a ride back into town. No one knows that I was with them!"

He was silent for a time and then he said: "Three of my people were arrested last night. They know."

"They don't know who I am. They probably assume that I was just an embassy official, like Grogan and Brecht and Datone and Alicia. They don't *know* that I'm Jim Racine, the fighter. They don't know that. I could appear in town this morning and no one would even think that I had been involved in this."

He frowned, chewed on his lower lip. "I think I called you by name yesterday."

"The chances are that your friends didn't even notice."

"Your picture has been in the newspaper, Racine."

"Even so, you've got a promise of twenty-four hours before your comrades talk to the police. That's plenty of time to get the money."

"How do you know about the twenty-four hours?"

"Don't ask me to use up part of my minute explaining."

"You're already into the second minute. Tell me."

"Grogan crawled down the tunnel this morning. He heard you talking."

Raoul stared down at me. He was thinking, he was considering the money.

"You have to run," I said. "You know you do. How much money do you have? How long do you think it will take to receive the ransom for the ambassador and Alicia Phillips? The U.S. government will probably refuse to pay you ransom. You'll have to get the money from the families of Fox and Alicia. That will take time, negotiation, care. Raoul, listen, I have thirteen thousand dollars. That's enough to give you a shot at getting away with this. Without that money you're dead, and you know it. How far can you get without money? Where can you hide, and for how long?"

He nodded slowly. "You propose to simply walk into the bank and withdraw all your money?"

"Yes."

He suddenly grinned. "Well, why not? Wait here, Racine." He turned and began climbing up over the glacial rubble toward the cave. The Indian and the girl, Sara, came outside and they talked. I could hear the murmur of their voices, but none of the individual words.

Oso, the machine pistol casually held in one hand, looked down at me. He was disappointed that I had been reprieved. He appeared frustrated and angry, like a hungry man who has been shown a great platter of food and then had the food taken away. Oso was the kind of man who enjoyed killing; violence was a source of pleasure for him, a kind of psychic food. He needed violence, death. I had encountered men like Oso among the gamblers and hoodlums and psychopaths who comprise a certain percentage of the fight crowd.

The sun had not yet risen above the mountains, but the clouds now glowed fluorescently against the indigo sky. The wind blowing down off the glacier evaporated my sweat. I felt that I could not adjust my breathing rhythm; either I hyperventilated and became dizzy from an excess of oxygen, or I breathed too shallowly and became oxygen starved. It was partly the effects of the altitude, but mostly it was due to fear—I had come very close to dying a few minutes ago, and they might choose to kill me a few minutes from now.

Oso was smoking a cigarette. Beyond him the others—Raoul, the girl, and the Indian—were still talking. Raoul gestured, shook his head, cut off an argument from Sara with a slice of his palm. Beyond and above them a hawk slowly corkscrewed up into the sky, riding an early-morning thermal.

"Racine!" Raoul shouted. "Come up here!"

I walked up the talus slope, passed Oso, who then followed me to the cave.

"I'm going to make a deal with you, Racine," Raoul said.

I nodded.

"You're going into the city with Tono and my sister. They won't be armed. Do you understand? All you have to do is walk up to the first policeman you see. They can do nothing to stop you. But, Racine, listen—if you betray them, the ambassador and Grogan and Miss Phillips will be killed. I don't know if that means anything to you. It may be that you value your own life too highly to care what happens to the others. The choice is yours.

But believe it, if my sister doesn't contact me according to the schedule we've arranged, the people in there"—he gestured toward the cave—"are dead."

"I understand."

"Do you? Perhaps you do. If you do understand, Racine, then you'll obey Sara's orders. You'll do as she says."

"Okay."

"I don't know if you're a man of honor, but I warn you that—"

"Let's not talk about honor," I said. "You've told me what my side of the bargain is. What do I receive in exchange?"

"Your life."

"Raoul, you gave me my life last night and then took it back this morning."

"Your life, and the lives of your three countrymen."

"How can I trust you?" I asked.

"How can I trust *you?*"

"It may be that I have a conscience," I said.

"I hope you do. You also have my sister."

"If I had a choice I wouldn't take her."

She grinned fiercely at me.

"You don't *have* to accept the offer, Racine," Raoul said. "You and Oso can walk back down the hill."

"I accept," I said.

He nodded and smiled. "I thought you would."

TWELVE

The girl, Tono—I assumed that "Tono" was a diminutive of Antonio—and I walked single file down the gravelly mountain path. The sun was warm on my back. Other volcanoes in the sierra were sharply defined by sun and sky. Far below I could see the cubical white houses of the village; wood smoke arose from every chimney, was spread and flattened by the wind, and covered the valley with a transparent blue haze.

A battered 1953 Chevrolet was parked next to the red truck. I sat in the rear seat with the girl. Tono backed the car out and then began to slowly drive down the rutted, potholed switchbacks toward the valley.

He kept the car in low gear and pumped the brakes from time to time. I could smell the brakes burning and hear the grating of metal against metal. Another well-maintained vehicle of the Revolution. Tono was a thin boy, not more than eighteen or nineteen, with a flat Indian face and Indian-black hair cut across his forehead in uneven bangs. He hummed softly to himself as he drove.

Sara was quiet. Her eyes still burned as madly as ever, but her mouth was sullen.

"I met your grandfather last week," I said. "The old man is your grandfather, isn't he?"

"He told us that you'd met," she said.

"He boasted about his grandchildren, you and Raoul. I wonder if he's as proud of you now."

"He's old, he doesn't understand what must be done." She spoke English well, though she had had trouble aspirating the English *H* sound.

"You shouldn't have involved him in this," I said.

Her eyebrows touched in a frown. "He isn't involved."

"Of course he is."

"He doesn't know what this is about."

"He probably has a pretty good idea by now."

"Be quiet," she said.

"Do you think that the police or military will believe that he's not involved?"

She did not reply.

"You might have considered the possibility that some of you would be arrested and interrogated. Jesus, Sara, why didn't you leave him out of this mess?"

"He was not supposed to be at the cave. He had said that he would visit town for several days."

"You're careless people."

"Shut up," she said.

"You're amateurs. Amateurs, hell—you're dilettantes. What did you think of the killings yesterday?"

"They were necessary."

"You don't believe that."

She turned and looked out the side window.

"The murders made you sick. Could you kill me, Sara?"

"Oh, yes," she said. "Easily."

"I don't think so. You're a parlor revolutionary. All of you are except Oso. Killing sounds easy when it's an abstraction, something you discuss late at night over coffee and cigarettes, but it's ugly. You saw how ugly it was."

"They were soldiers," she said.

"Then they should have been taken prisoner, not shot down like rabid dogs."

"And what do you think will happen to us if we're captured?" she said bitterly. "What do you think is happening to our comrades now? Do you think they're being treated according to the Geneva Convention rules? I'll tell you what will happen to me if I am stupid enough not to commit suicide before they capture me. For the first day or two, only the officers will rape and abuse me. Then the noncommissioned officers. Then whoever remains—privates, recruits, the janitor, the criminal prisoners. Many of them would certainly have peculiar tastes.

"You," she said softly, contemptuously. "You talk about the ugliness of the killing yesterday. Those men did not suffer long. But I would suffer, oh yes, I would suffer. As our comrades are suffering right now. You call us terrorists. The real terrorists in this country are working in the government palace and in all of the police stations and military barracks. We are amateurs, you say. Yes, it is true, we are amateurs in terror. We will get a million dollars in ransom from your noble ambassador and his slut. And with that money we'll recruit fighters, and buy arms, and we'll learn how to be professional terrorists."

"And you'll become just as bad as them."

"Of course," she said. "Worse, much worse. Do you think we are going to win because we have beautiful souls? We shall win through hatred, viciousness, terror. They will learn to fear *us*."

"I suppose they will," I said.

"Those men yesterday, those soldiers. They were our enemy. Your country is our enemy. You give money and arms and advice to the perverted fascist scum who govern this land. Your State Department becomes hysterical if there is any talk of truly democratic elections. Your CIA, working with the government, have destroyed the trade-union movement, prevented land reform, assassinated or imprisoned or exiled every political leader to the left of Adolf Hitler, helped to maintain peasants in actual slavery to the Church and oligarchs—and you tell me that the killing of those two American soldiers was ugly. There will be more killing, more ugliness. You have a saying, fight fire with fire. Yes. And torture with torture, and murder with murder, and terror with terrorism. Is there anything else you want to know?"

"Yes. In the future, how can I avoid these Revolutionary tirades?"

"By declining to give me lectures in bourgeois morality."

There was a roadblock a mile outside the city limits of Quitasol. The car was searched, we were questioned and required to show identification, and permitted to pass. Both Sara and the Indian seemed very nervous. That was all right, she said later: the citizens were expected to be nervous when in the company of police; a lack of nervousness would have been suspicious. The policemen recognized me. It was true, then, that it was not known that I had been with the ambassador during the kidnapping. And the police were obviously not yet looking for Sara and Tono.

It was only eight-thirty, and the bank would not open for another ninety minutes, and so I suggested that we go to my hotel, where I could shower and shave and change into clean clothes.

Sara hesitated.

"I don't think it's a good idea for me to walk into the bank looking like a tramp and withdraw thirteen thousand dollars."

She shook her head.

"It will be safer for you in the hotel than prowling around the city in this old junk of a car."

"All right," she said.

Tono found a parking place on a side street near the hotel. The girl told him to make the telephone calls that Raoul had mentioned, and meet us back at the car at ten o'clock.

The desk clerk looked at my soiled clothes and two-day beard, glanced at Sara, who was not much neater, smiled lewdly, and made a soft clicking sound with his tongue. He gave me my room key and a note from Nacho.

Jimmy:

Where the hell have you been, 'Mano? Call me right away. We got the Barboa fight if you will accept a little less money.

NACHO C.

That's the way it always was: No one ever asked you to accept a little *more* money.

"That policeman has been waiting for you," the desk clerk said. "He's over there."

"What policeman?" Sara asked hoarsely.

"It's okay," I told her.

The desk clerk smirked at us and turned back to his newspaper.

Emilio Durán was dozing openmouthed in a white leather chair. I started toward him.

"What are you doing?" Sara hissed. "What is this?"

"It's all right," I said.

Durán was sweating even though the lobby was cool. He wore the same baggy suit, the same frayed, dirty shirt, but he had bought a new pair of patent leather shoes with two-inch heels. I touched his shoulder and his teeth snapped together and his arms and legs twitched; he looked like a dog who had been dreaming about chasing rabbits.

"You bastard," Sara said softly, viciously.

I touched Durán again and he sat up straight in the chair. He stared blankly at me for a moment and then smiled tentatively, yawned, permitted the smile to return.

"You've been waiting for me?" I asked.

"What? Oh, yes."

"Is there anything wrong?"

He glanced at Sara with his dark, sorrowful eyes and then slowly got to his feet. He was fat enough so that he had to rock back and forth a couple of times before gaining the momentum to arise. He reached inside his jacket and for an instant I feared that he intended to draw a gun, but then he withdrew my passport.

"I've been instructed to return this to you," he said.

I accepted it, opened it and looked it over. "Thank you."

"I waited for you most of yesterday and all last night."

"I was out in the country," I said.

He looked at Sara.

"This is María Ramírez," I said, quickly inventing a name.

Sara showed him her murderous, hot-eyed, teeth-locked grin.

"Thank you for delivering the passport," I said.

"Yes, it was a long wait. I neglected other, more important duties to insure that it was promptly returned to you."

"Were you told why the police decided to give it back to me?"

"No." He sighed deeply. "I am fatigued from the long wait."

I understood what he wanted. "Would you permit me to buy you a fine dinner to repay you for your difficulties?"

He nodded. "I think that would be acceptable."

I reached for my wallet.

Durán quickly raised his palms. "Not here. People might not understand a simple gesture of gratitude."

We walked over to the elevator area and I gave him twenty dollars worth of local currency. He seemed disappointed. I threw in another five dollars and he went away.

"He seems rather gentle, don't you think?" I said to Sara when the elevator doors hissed shut. "Not exactly your typical perverted fascist scum."

"He's corrupt."

"He's that," I said. "I'm going to try to claim him as a dependent on my income-tax return."

"The man is respectful to you, yes. You have money and are well known here and have a powerful embassy protecting you. But I wonder how many peasants he has beaten. I wonder how many poor girls he has molested. Do you think he is equally humble to the people in the *barrios* who can't pay bribes?"

I phoned the desk from my room and asked to have two breakfasts of eggs, bacon, toast, orange juice, and coffee sent up; then I took a change of clothes into the bathroom, showered, shaved, and dressed. The breakfasts had arrived and Sara was eating when I returned to the room. I sat down across from her at the small table.

"Why didn't you tell the police?" she said. "You had two opportunities, at the roadblock and downstairs. Why didn't you tell them?"

"Because your brother and Oso would kill three innocent people."

"You are one of God's noblemen," she said.

I smiled at her. "If it were just Ambassador Fox and Grogan . . . "

"You'd let them die?"

"Maybe, if it would get my neck out of the noose."

She finished her breakfast and stood up. "Does this hotel have a clothing shop?"

"I think it does. Yes."

"I'm going to order some clothes sent up. Do you have money?"

"I have a small checking account that I forgot to mention to Raoul. What the hell—I'll throw that into the kitty, too."

She telephoned the desk clerk and had him switch her to the boutique. She gave very crisp and precise instructions as to her sizes and preferences in style and color, and then hung up. Fifteen minutes later a saleswoman, followed by two porters carrying armloads of clothing, came into the room. Sara quarreled with them, angrily criticized the quality and prices, and finally bought three skirts, a pants suit, half a dozen blouses, several pairs of shoes, a cocktail dress, an alligator handbag, and a swimming suit. The bill came to eight hundred and forty-three dollars.

"I'm glad you're a revolutionary ascetic," I said. "If you were petit bourgeois I'd be destitute now."

"You are destitute," she said. "Remember? You traded your ten-peso life for your fortune."

She sat down at the vanity and began hacking at her hair with scissors. She did everything with a kind of sulky fury, even cutting her hair. It looked like a kind of dreadful self-mutilation, but when she had finished her hair was cut in a short ragged style that a fashion magazine would probably call saucy or piquant. Then she rapidly, carelessly plucked her thick eyebrows into a thin, arched line, applied mascara, lipstick, and blue eye shadow. She got up and walked across the room with an exaggerated, hippy, pelvic-thrusting way, drawing her lips together in a pout and sucking in her cheeks. "Regard your wife," she said.

"My ex-wife would have showered *before* putting on her makeup," I said.

"Your ex-wife is probably an over-sanitary bitch."

"She is, in fact."

"Pack your belongings."

"Where are we going?"

"To the sea coast for a holiday, darling."

"I can use a holiday."

"But you will tell the desk that were going to a spa in the mountains. I am your American hygienic bitch of a wife, joining you for a gala, colorful South American vacation."

"Everyone will believe that."

"Pay your bill, tip everyone excessively, even that vile desk clerk."

"Okay, Sara."

"From now on I am—what was your wife's name?"

"Nancy."

"I am Nancy Racine."

"And I am a two-time loser," I said.

Tono was waiting for us in the car. We drove to the bank and I withdrew all of the money in accordance to Sara's instructions: five thousand dollars in the local currency, three thousand in Brazilian cruzeiros, and the rest in dollars.

The bank officer seemed to be suffering from extreme anxiety as he dealt the money across the counter, and he suggested that I convert most of it into traveler's checks or a cashier's draft. I told him that it was mad money for my wife and it wouldn't last long enough to be exposed to theft.

Sara gave most of the money to Tono and stuck the rest in her new alligator handbag. He dropped us off at a car-rental agency.

"You know what Raoul wants," Sara said to him.

He nodded.

"*Suerte*, Tono," she said, and she embraced him and kissed his cheek.

We rented a new Dodge and drove down off the *altiplano* to the coast for our honeymoon.

THIRTEEN

The resort of Las Playas Sureste was built on the sandstone cliffs overlooking the clear, neon-blue water of Bahía Tranquilidad. Tranquility Bay—it had a nice sound. I was told by some fishermen that for hundreds of years it had been known as Bahía Tiburón, Shark Bay; but the investors who had built the hotel believed that their guests needed tranquility more than they needed sharks, and so the name had been changed. The fishermen told me that for six months they had earned extra money by hanging up the biggest sharks they could catch on the village pier, and then accepting money from the hotel management to dispose of the carcasses. Finally a law was passed forbidding the public display of any part of a shark. You could actually go to jail now for wearing a shark's-tooth bracelet or being caught in the possession of a shark's liver. The fishermen did not know of any tourists who had been attacked by sharks in the eighteen months that the hotel had been operating. They joked about going out early in the morning and chumming the water off the hotel's private beach. A couple hundred pounds of fish guts would do it. "That hotel needs more one-legged guests," a man called "Noodles" told me. I bought them a round of drinks and made them promise to notify me of the day when they chummed the water.

The hotel architecture was a bastard hybrid of Inca masonry and Hilton glass; it looked like it had been designed by a schizophrenic computer. But the cabañas were comfortable, the food good, the service not quite insolent, the sun hot, and the water of the bay refreshingly cool. The guests—about one third from the United States and Europe, the rest from Latin America—were all very old. Perhaps only old people and kidnapped prizefighters could afford the prices. Everyone seemed to have calfless legs and big buttocks and burnt-sienna tans. They did not like us, although a couple from Los Angeles were friendly enough to fleece Sara and me of one hundred and thirty dollars at bridge.

Sara hated them, of course. She hated everyone, including the native servant staff, who had chosen to carry trays and laundry instead of hand grenades. She burned them to ashes with her eyes; and she locked her teeth together in that crazy, fierce grin. And she was hated in return.

Waiters quarreled about whose turn it was to serve our table. Not even the Los Angeles couple, certain of winning at least another hundred and thirty dollars, invited us back for a bridge game. Sara was almost always grim, offensively direct, intolerant, searching for injustice as if it were a cockroach that got into the sugar bowl every night. She had the self-righteousness of an inquisitor and the temper of a wolverine. Sara was a dictator looking for a population to oppress.

We had registered at the hotel as Mr. and Mrs. Racine. At rare moments she became frivolous and tried to behave as she thought a spoiled American woman might. I did not recognize anything specifically American in her parody. She puffed out her lips and sulked; she whirled, spinning her skirt like a bullfighter's cape; she walked like a three-dollar tart, all rotation, hips and pelvis and shoulders and rear; and when the mood of satire overwhelmed her she spent money on completely useless things like teddy bears, ridiculously expensive seashell ashtrays, boats made out of toothpicks, porcelain castles, big-eyed squid knitted out of colored yarn. Sara believed that she was mocking American women, but I found out the American women in the hotel called her "Carmen Miranda." She was considered a classically suitable wife for a professional fighter.

Every night before dinner I waited in the lobby while she carried a double handful of change into a pay telephone booth and called Raoul.

The newspapers carried front-page stories of the kidnappings: suspects were being questioned; the police and military investigators were following some important leads; there had been no response from the U.S. State Department concerning the ransom demand of one million dollars, although it was known that the families of Ambassador Fox and Miss Alicia Phillips were presently negotiating with the kidnappers; an American spokesman vehemently denied that Daniel Grogan was employed by the CIA; the police demanded new powers to deal with terrorists and kidnappers.

"It doesn't sound as though your captured friends have talked," I said.

"Oh, they've talked by now," Sara said. "The police know who we are."

"Aren't you frightened?"

"The police aren't looking for Mrs. James Racine. And Raoul and Oso and Tono are safe."

"Where? Where are they now?"

"They're safe."

"Still, aren't you frightened?"

"God, yes," she whispered, and then she licked her lips and grinned at me as if I were an apple.

If Sara had told me where Fox, Grogan, and Alicia were being held, I would have considered turning her in to the police or military, who might have been able to mount some sort of commando action which could save those three lives—and my life. I had purchased my life from Raoul twice: once, unknowingly, for a two-dollar plate of food, and then for thirteen thousand dollars. I could not afford to ransom myself again in Raoul's inflationary market. And there was really nothing I could do at the moment unless I was willing to sacrifice three lives in order to secure my own. I believed that Raoul would kill the captives if Sara missed one of her telephone calls.

We stayed at the resort for five days. We followed the same schedule each day: breakfast in our cabaña at eight; four hours on the beach, sunning and swimming; lunch in the hotel dining room, and then a long nap; a walk through the village at dusk and a drink at each of three bars; back to the hotel again to shower and change for dinner; a long, slow, too-heavy meal with too much wine; an after-dinner drink at the bar and then to the cabaña for sleep. I was eating too much, drinking too much, and I enjoyed it as you can only enjoy those things which make you feel guilty afterwards.

Our room had twin beds. The beds were just a few feet apart; I could hear her breathing at night, hear her turn, murmur softly. She smelled of sun and the salt sea. I thought about sex, of course. I don't think I thought of anything else.

Sara appeared slender in clothing and then full-figured, almost heavy in a bikini or naked. She was either totally indifferent to her body or deliberately provocative. The latter, I'm sure. She often removed her bikini after swimming and walked around the room nude for fifteen or twenty minutes, ordering lunch from the desk, reading a magazine, combing her hair, oiling her sundried body, resting on the bed. I considered her casual nakedness an invitation: I went to her, and was clubbed on my eye with a roundhouse right.

"You're just a goddamned tease," I said angrily.

She said that she would not pollute herself with the enemy.

"Then stop exhibiting yourself to the enemy."

But she continued to perform her striptease two or three times a day.

On the morning of the fourth day I asked, "How much longer will we be staying here?"

"Guess."

"I don't *know.*"

She grinned smugly.

"The money is running low," I said.

On the morning of the fifth day she received a long-distance telephone call in the room. I assumed it was from Raoul, although she did not call him by name. "Yes," she said. "Yes. No. Tomorrow? Yes, I know where it is. No. No, he hasn't. He's stupid," she said, and she slanted an evil glance toward me from under her brows. "Yes." She laughed. "Café Piña, yes. Goodbye."

She was in a triumphant mood after that, and we did not return to the hotel for lunch, but bought beer and clams from a peddler on the beach. We didn't go to our cabaña until four o'clock that afternoon. Sara stripped off her bikini and paced back and forth across the room, pausing twice to look at her body in the mirror. The marks of her bikini were two small strips of white against the sunburn. We were both sunburned, taut-skinned from sun and sea, heat-drugged, drowsy and tense at the same time.

"I want a drink," Sara said.

I ordered some ice and when it arrived I made two gin and tonics.

"We're leaving tonight," Sara said.

"Where are we going?"

"Refugio. Isn't that appropriate?"

"I don't know the place," I said.

"Everything is going well now."

"Is it?"

"We have help now from some very important people and an important organization."

"When am I going to be released?"

"I don't know." She held her glass in both hands, like a child, tilted back her head and drank deeply.

"You crazy bitch," I said.

She looked at me.

"Put on some clothes."

"Does it bother you?"

"It's a distraction."

She sat on the edge of the bed for a moment, then lay back.

I removed my swimming suit and approached her. She watched me without expression.

"Hit me," I said. "I've got another eye."

But she welcomed me. We came together in an act that could not be described as love; it was a violent collision of bodies and egos. We sought to dominate, subdue each other through a sex that was like war. We stayed in the bed for two hours. And each time there was less rage in us until finally, surprisingly, we found—not love certainly, not even affection—but a calm that transcended satiety. She was a strange girl, this Sara. And she turned my perspective and made me recognize a strangeness in myself.

PART THREE
RIVERS

FOURTEEN

We checked out of the hotel at nine that night and arrived in Refugio at eleven the following morning. It was an exhausting drive over dangerously narrow roads which rapidly gained and lost altitude. Often there was a sheer two-thousand-foot drop just beyond the edge of pavement and absolutely no place to hide if a big truck should come blasting out from behind a curve. The trip was divided into three steps: from sea level up to Quitasol at 9,400 feet; the extremely hazardous section from the *altiplano* to a 16,000-foot pass; and then down the eastern flank of the Andes into the tropics. It was very cold in the really high country and there were patches of dirty snow alongside the road.

Sara slept most of the way. I nibbled at sandwiches that had been prepared by the hotel kitchen and sipped coffee from a Thermos. The moon and shadows turned the mountains into a surrealist landscape, made it look like a terrain forgotten from an old dream and now vaguely remembered. I had never seen so many stars. And stars, simple stars, had never made me feel anxious before.

Well down the eastern slope I drove into a layer of humid heat; it was like abruptly moving from a refrigerator into a sauna. Within a few minutes I was sweating. There were new, rich odors on the wind, and the stars receded in the humidity-blurred sky.

Refugio was a dirty, foul-smelling river town of about twenty thousand people on the west bank of the Río Fuerte—the Strong River. It didn't look very strong at this point. It was about one hundred yards wide, quite deep (you could tell it was deep by the heavily silent way it flowed), and ocherous with mud. The surface was lightly touched with whorls and dimples and, in the shallow water along the bank, long chevrons of ripples. The river looked viscid, halfway between a liquid and a solid. And it exhaled a disagreeable chemical stink. The area around the town had been cleared of timber and brush, but across the river I could see the tall green rain forest.

The wooden shacks along the river were built on stilts. This was the rainy season, the river was rising and had already climbed halfway up the stilts. Behind the shacks, on semi-dry ground, pigs and chickens and skeletal dogs and potbellied children played together. Vultures perched in ranks on all the rooftops and in the few remaining trees; they looked like gloomy clerics.

Only a few of the town's streets were paved, the rest were made out of packed dirt the color of the river. Refugio. Some refuge. Mud, heat, humidity, clouds of black gnats, shrewd-looking vultures, children with their bellies swollen with worms, a nostril-burning stink of decay.

I turned the Dodge around at the river and started back toward the main section of town.

"Sara," I said. "Wake up."

She stirred, murmured something in Spanish, and then her eyelids fluttered open and she stared at me without recognition.

"We're home, honey," I said, smiling at her.

She stared at me for a moment longer and then I could see depth and light enter her eyes. She slowly drew herself erect and looked through the windshield.

"Where are we?" she asked in a sleep-coarsened voice.

"Refugio."

"This is Refugio?"

"This is it."

"What time is it?"

"A little after eleven."

"Oh, God, were late. Go directly to the Café Piña."

"That's fine, but where is the Café Piña?"

"We'll stop and ask someone. There, ask that man on the corner."

"He's a policeman."

"Ask someone else, then," she said crossly. "Must I do all your thinking for you?"

"I know I'm not as cool, clear-eyed, and lucid as you are, Sara. That's why you're part of this brilliantly executed coup and I'm a mere prisoner."

"Just shut up and find the café."

"You're the smartest girl I've ever met who's going to die by firing squad."

She locked her teeth and grinned. "I can promise you that I'll outlive you no matter how soon I die."

The Café Piña was located on a narrow side street between a tobacco shop and a pharmacy. Decals advertising various brands of beer and cigarettes were pasted to the filthy windows, and a signboard above the door—CAFÉ PIÑA—lay askew, secured now by one rusty hinge.

Inside was a small room, perhaps forty feet by twenty, with some wooden tables and chairs, a counter, an exposed grill, a pair of slowly revolving ceiling fans, and half a dozen flyspecked soccer posters pinned to the walls. Flies meticulously washed their wings and legs on the table tops and buzzed sluggishly against the plate-glass windows. The place smelled of rancid animal fats. There were no customers; they had all probably died of food poisoning a long time ago.

We sat at a table next to the window. Flies were crawling like black maggots through the sugar in the open bowl.

"Just the right place for a clandestine meeting," I said.

"He's not here," Sara said. "We're late, he's gone."

"Who are we looking for?"

"A man."

A short, hairy man who wore a red plastic apron and a triangular hat fashioned out of a page from a newspaper emerged from the back room and laid two hand-lettered menus in front of us without disturbing the flies.

Sara glanced at the menu. "I'm starved," she said.

"Try the pork, Sara. Ham or bacon. The pork in this place will kill you faster than the bite from a fer-de-lance."

She smiled faintly. "I don't suppose the eggs can give you botulism."

"That depends on what they're fried in."

"I'll have a Coca Cola," she said.

I ordered a Coke and a bottle of beer from the chef-maître d'-waiter.

We sat quietly for about twenty minutes, sipping our drinks, and then the door opened and a very tall, very thin man entered the café. He glanced at us, kicked the door shut with his heel, walked to a table in the back of the room, and sat down.

"Is that him?" I asked.

"I don't know."

The man removed a newspaper from the side pocket of his suit jacket, carefully unfolded and smoothed it, and began reading. His thin gray face looked like it had been fashioned out of wax, left out in the sun, where it partially melted, and then taken back indoors to harden. His nose, ears, and chin were long and pointed, his mouth sagged at the corners, his eyes were deeply sunken into his skull.

I ordered another beer.

After a few minutes another man entered the café, a middle-aged black man with prematurely white steel-wool hair, a thin white moustache, and rose-tinted gold-frame aviator-style glasses. His left leg was frozen at the knee and he half limped, half dragged it behind him as he walked to the counter.

I looked at Sara. She shrugged.

The man ordered a cup of coffee and then withdrew a pencil and a small notebook. He wrote steadily in the notebook, pausing to moisten the pencil lead with his tongue.

Now the wax man at the back of the room rolled his newspaper into a tube, slapped it against his open palm a couple of times, as if preparing to beat a dog.

I heard a harsh grating noise and looked out the window. A legless man with a string of blue lottery tickets in his teeth glided along the sidewalk on a kind of skateboard, a plank with roller-skate wheels fixed to the bottom. He used his hands as oars, gliding swiftly backwards, looking over his left shoulder, the wheels clicking on the sidewalk cracks. I could still hear the noise after he passed out of sight.

I had finished my second beer and was starting on the third when the black man arose from his stool, using the counter edge for leverage, and then limped across the room and stood above us. He was smiling.

"Sara?" he asked.

"Yes," she said.

The man sat down between Sara and me.

"You're late," he said softly.

"I know. I'm sorry."

"Racine," he said to me.

I nodded.

"Have you been a good boy, Racine?"

"Butter wouldn't melt in my mouth," I said.

He smiled at me. He had a smile that any politician or psychiatrist would give an arm for. I see you, his smile said, I know all about you, and I like you anyway.

He turned and spoke to Sara in what at first sounded like a queerly accented Spanish; but after a moment I realized that he was speaking Portuguese. A Brazilian? Sara seemed to have no difficulty understanding him, although she replied in Spanish. "No," she said. "Yes," she said. "I'm sorry, truly I am." She appeared ashamed, meeker than I ever expected to see her.

I sipped my beer. The wax man in the rear of the café had his eyes closed, his head tilted back, as if he were taking the sun. He smiled to himself. His mouth turned down at the corners when he smiled.

The black man switched back to English. "You people were very, very stupid, Sara," he said gently.

"I know. We—I'm sorry."

"If you had consulted the Party . . . "

"Please, it was only . . . I'm sorry." She was very unhappy.

"Raoul would have been *very* valuable if he had remained at the American embassy. What was he thinking of? What were *you* thinking of, Sara?"

She looked down at her hands.

"Well, never mind, it's over now. We're going to help you."

She raised her eyes and smiled tentatively, gratefully.

"Where is the rented car, Sara?"

"Outside. It's parked down the street."

"The red Dodge?"

"Yes." Her smile flickered on and off as she watched his face for clues to his mood.

I didn't like seeing her this way. Without her courage she was nothing.

"All right," the man said. "Let's go, Sara." He stood up, bearing his weight on his good, right leg.

"Yes," she said, and she was smiling without qualification now. He spoke to her as if she were a lost child, and she seemed to like it; she responded with a sleepy, almost drugged obedience.

They walked together to the door. He opened it and then paused, looking back at me. "Aren't you coming, Racine?"

"No," I said. "You can just buzz off without me."

"Are you sure?"

"I've fulfilled my half of the agreement," I said. "I've given my money and my cooperation. I'm through. Goodbye and good luck."

He gestured to Sara, she passed through the door, and he followed. I watched them walk past the window. Sara walked slowly, so that he would have no difficulty keeping up with her.

The wax man approached my table. The newspaper, folded in half, covered his right hand. He lifted the forward edge and showed me the muzzle of a pistol.

I got up from the table and preceded him through the door.

FIFTEEN

I drove and Sara sat in the front seat next to me; the two men were in back. We followed a paved road three miles south of town and then the pavement abruptly ended and we continued down a narrow muddy strip that ran as straight as a rhumb line through the rain forest. Tire ruts were filled with water that glowed a pale gold in the sunlight.

"Another week of rains and it will be impossible to travel this road," the black man said conversationally.

"Yes," Sara said, and she smiled. Her features seemed to have smoothed out, she looked younger, and her eyes no longer burned. She was pleased to have been freed of responsibility. This smiling fatherly man made her feel safe; everything would be all right now. She was a fool.

I glanced out the side window. The rain forest began just a few feet away and I could look into it. I saw great hardwood trees that trailed flowering lianas and vines as thick as a ship's hawser, filmy green veils of moss, many kinds of palms, some no taller than a child and others arching up out of sight into the high foliage.

After about twenty minutes I was ordered to stop the car.

"Turn here," the man said.

"Where?"

"Here, to the left."

"There's no road, for Christ's sake."

"Turn between those two big trees."

I twisted the steering wheel and drove slowly between the trees. Branches and ferns lashed against the windshield, we were totally immersed in green for a moment, and then we passed through the outer barrier and entered the rain forest. The tree trunks were widely spaced and there was far less ground shrubbery than I would have supposed, probably because so little sunlight penetrated the thick weave of leaves high overhead. We were submerged in a kind of green mist. It was dusk here, going on night. A hundred feet inside the forest I saw the red truck. The man told me to park behind it. I turned off the ignition.

"Is Raoul here?" Sara asked.

"Yes. Raoul is here. Everyone is here."

"Where are they?"

"That way, down by the river. You're going to take a river journey, Sara."

"Are you coming?"

"No, but I'll see you again in about ten days."

We got out of the car. It was hot and quiet and very humid in the forest, like a greenhouse; the air was blurry with humidity and the car was already beginning to fog with condensation.

The man, limping slowly, led us toward the east. Sara and I followed him; the wax man remained about twenty feet behind us. The soil was wet and loamy. The air was rich with the odors of living and decaying vegetation. There were perfect palm trees, huge lacy ferns, dangling masses of parisitical vegetation, clumps of moss, sixty-foot-long lianas that looked as if they had been made of steel wire and symmetrical shards of green glass, tree trunks ten feet in diameter, orchids as big as my head, iridescent hummingbirds that flashed like jewels. All of the various shades of green blended together into a single misty, diffused underwater light—the rain forest was as you might imagine the bottom of the sea.

My clothes were almost immediately soaked with sweat; I could taste salt, and salt sweat burned my eyes. We walked for about fifteen minutes and then suddenly broke through into a natural clearing. I saw tents, hammocks strung from trees, piles of supplies, two rubber rafts, one very large and the other very small, and people—I saw the ambassador, Alicia Phillips, Grogan; and at the other end of the clearing, Raoul, Oso, the Indian boy, the old man. They all stared at us when we entered the area. Oso lowered his machine pistol. Raoul grinned, said, *"Bienvenidos."*

Sara hurried across the clearing and embraced her brother. When they separated I could see that she was crying.

I could smell and hear, but not see, the river.

"Racine," the smiling man said, "why don't you join your compatriots?"

The ambassador and Alicia were sitting on the ground in front of a pyramidal tent. They were wearing the same clothes they'd had on the day of the picnic; Fox, the fishnet shirt, chocolate-brown slacks, and brown and white spiked golf shoes; Alicia, a white blouse and blue skirt, blue low-heeled shoes. Their clothing was soiled and wrinkled now, their hair matted, and the ambassador had six days of beard stubble on his cheeks. And there was a bloodstained bandage wrapped around his right hand and wrist.

I walked over and smiled down at them. "Hi," I said. "Small rain forest."

Fox looked up at me without recognition. He looked bad; his eyes were dead, his skin gray, the lines around his mouth and eyes had deepened, and there was a hint of deep apathy about his stillness. He behaved like a man in shock.

"Are you all right, Ambassador?" I asked.

He did not reply. He stared up at me. His eyes possessed a dullness I had seen many times before; they were like the eyes of a man who has just been knocked out but has not yet fallen.

"Thank you," Alicia said to me.

"For what?"

"You could have saved yourself."

"I wouldn't miss this for anything, Alicia. This is what the newspapers will call an adventure when we're freed."

She tried to smile. I wondered if this was the first time in her adult life that she had not been elegantly bathed, perfumed, coiffed, and dressed.

"I'll go over and say hello to Dan," I said.

"Yes," she said. "Thank you," she said. "Jim, thank you."

Dan Grogan was sitting crosslegged on the ground about thirty yards away from Fox and Alicia. His clothes were soiled too. The humidity had turned his curly red hair into a pulpy mass that looked like a sponge, and his six-day beard glinted like copper wire in the sunlight. But his eyes were still as cold and clear a green as before, and there was tension in his jaw.

He grinned up at me. "Have a prurient time, *amigo?*"

"How is it going, Dan?"

"Guess," he said. And then: "Listen, Racine, you must be a victim of *dementia pugilistica.*"

"What's that?"

"That's a tactful way of saying that you're punch-drunk. Why didn't you run when you had the chance?"

"Would you have run?"

"I'll tell you exactly what I would have done. I would have punched out that Sara bitch and dragged her by the hair to the nearest police station."

"If I had done that you'd be dead now."

He shrugged. "If positions had been reversed you'd be dead now, chum."

I sat down and leaned back against a rotten log.

"Don't touch that. It's filled with red ants that have a bite worse than a wasp's sting."

I quickly moved away from the log. "Why aren't you over there with Fox and Alicia?" I said.

"Because I can't stand her brave-martyr pose, and I can't stand the whipped-dog look in his eyes."

"What happened to his hand?"

"Oso cut off four of his fingers. He left the thumb, though."

"*What?*"

Grogan grinned. "Yesterday morning."

"Christ, Grogan."

"I warned Fox, I told him to shut his goddamned mouth, but he wouldn't listen. The pigheaded Rotarian fool! He thought nothing bad could happen to him. He thought he was America, and they wouldn't dare harm America. Oso got tired of his pompous, righteous indignation, and he told Fox to shut up. But the ambassador wasn't afraid of these scum, you see, none of this was *real* to him, and so Fox told Oso in Spanish—I didn't know he could put together three words in Spanish—he told Oso that he, Oso, was a shameless son of a whore, and then he *spit* on Oso. I mean, man, my God, that cheapjack, potbellied manufacturer of glue spit on our psychopathic Oso! Jesus, it was beautiful and horrible to see."

"What happened, Grogan?"

"Oso grabbed Fox's wrist, pinned his hand to the ground, whipped out a knife half the size of a machete, and chopped off four fingers. Oso let go of his wrist then. Fox looked down for a moment, like he was puzzled, and then he lifted his hand and looked at it. His fingers remained on the ground, naturally. And the blood gushed out and Fox began screaming. We managed to stop the bleeding eventually. Fox hasn't been the same since, though. As you can see."

"Couldn't Raoul stop it?"

"It happened fast. Anyway, Raoul is afraid of Oso. So am I. So is the ambassador now—he starts trembling every time Oso comes within twenty feet. Raoul needed a tough guy and he got Oso. Oso is in this thing for the bucks."

"Who are those two new characters?"

"The spade is a big man in the Brazilian C.P. His name is Dos Santos. I've seen a dossier on him. The other guy—I don't know. Did he speak Portuguese?"

"No, he didn't speak at all."

"Nothing?"

"No, not a word."

"That's interesting. Maybe he's Cuban and doesn't want to give it away with his accent. Or, hell, he might even be a Russian. No, the Russians wouldn't get involved in this kind of fuck-up."

I looked across the clearing. Raoul and Dos Santos were separated from the others, talking quietly. Or rather, Dos Santos talked and Raoul listened and nodded his head. The old man was lying supine in the shade of a palm. I did not see Tono. Sara and the wax man were eating; they sat on the ground, their knees drawn up to support the metal plates. Oso, cradling his machine pistol as if it were a baby, stared at me until I averted my eyes. I glanced back briefly and saw that he was grinning at having so easily outstared me. I counted my fingers.

"You look like you had an easy time of it," Grogan said.

"First-class hotels and restaurants all the way."

"We lived like pigs in a stone hut. And traveled like pigs to market in the back of that truck."

"Grogan, just what is going on?"

He grinned. "You are about to embark on a thrilling river journey through the wilderness, pal. Try to enjoy it. Look at it this way—suckers in the States pay a thousand bucks to float the Colorado or the Snake, and this is a freebie for you."

"Like hell it's free. It's costing me thirteen thousand dollars."

"It may prove worth it, Racine. I've seen the topographical maps of the river ahead, and it drops like hell in places. Hang on. You'll be going through a canyon that's halfway between a pond and a waterfall."

"Will it be bad?"

"That's what I'm saying, chum."

"Does Raoul know how bad it will be?"

"No, he's a city kid. But I saw Dos Santos looking at the topos, and he expects you all to perish."

"Grogan, what is the point of going down the river?"

"Think about it, babe. Those people over there are hot, very hot. The airports and border exits are locked shut. But there are no border stations on the river. You can cross into Peru and only the monkeys will know."

"Peru!"

"Sure. You'll take the Fuerte for a day or so and then the Fuerte merges into the Loco. If you survive the

Fuerte, you can reach the Amazon below Inquitos. From there it's clear sailing into Brazil."

"Jesus Christ, Grogan."

He grinned and nodded vigorously. "That punk Raoul is an imaginative thinker."

"It looks that way."

"Trouble is you won't make it."

"You sound as if you don't intend to come with us," I said.

"Well, the fact is, I have a previous engagement."

"Yeah?"

"Dos Santos and his friend are taking me with them."

"Why?"

"They're going to debrief me."

"That doesn't sound good."

"It sounds better to me than the rivers."

"Are you going to talk to them?"

He shrugged. "I don't know. How can you say? At one point or another I might get the chance to escape or maybe kill those bastards—did you steal any sharp cutlery from one of those first-class restaurants? But if I can't get away, and if I fail to kill them, then maybe I'll talk. And maybe I won't. Maybe I'll feed them bits of information at a rate that will keep me alive well into senility."

"How much do you know, Dan?"

"I've been chief of station in Quitasol for almost two years. Before that I was deputy station chief in Bogotá. And before that I worked in Argentina. I know operations, I know names. Listen, I don't have to protect the regular CIA personnel. But there are people drawing money from us who are high in the trade unions, the Church, the C.P., the police, military, government—those are the ones I have to protect."

"Good luck," I said.

"It's going to rain again," Grogan said, looking up at the sky. "Look at my shoes. And my belt. Leather grows a nasty-looking fungus overnight in this climate."

"One more thing, Grogan."

"I've got a rash on my side that looks like it's ready to burst out in mushrooms."

"Dan . . . "

"Yeah?"

"You don't think we can make it down the river?"

"Oh, hell, you might. That big raft is tough. An experienced man could probably bring the big raft through all right. You may luck out."

"And you say that Dos Santos doesn't expect us to make it, that he'll be pleased if we don't get through."

"Sure. That will simplify everything. I figure that if he thought you had just a ten-percent chance of making it, he and his friend would kill all of you right now. *All of you.* Raoul, Sara, Oso, the Indian kid, the old man, Fox, Alicia, you too, Racine. You all can identify him. And he doesn't want the trouble of concealing those hot, bungling amateurs, and he most of all does not want to share the money."

"That's the point. How can they get the money if Fox and Alicia die on the river?"

Grogan smiled wryly. "You're refreshingly naïve, Racine."

"Maybe so."

"Big strong fellow like you—*dementia*. Look, Raoul thinks that Dos Santos and his people are going to save him from the grave he dug for himself. Dos Santos has taken over the negotiations for the ransom money. For two days now, we've—Fox, Alicia and me—have been talking into tape recorders. And they've taken photographs of us. Dos Santos will probably get the money, and you'll drown."

"Thanks, Dan."

"It's nothing," he said. "Have a good time."

At dusk, Dos Santos and the wax man took Grogan away.

"See you, kid," Grogan said. "Grow gills quick."

SIXTEEN

Birds awakened me at false dawn: they warbled, whistled, cawed, shrieked—it sounded more like static on a radio during a thunderstorm than the singing of birds. And then the sun rose and illuminated the green canopy overhead and began trickling down through the leaves to collect in small bright pools on the forest floor. It was hot and humid, even at this hour. Mosquitoes had penetrated the hammock netting and my arms and face were welted and streaked with blood.

After a breakfast of beans, rice, biscuits, and coffee, we began to break camp.

Raoul issued orders and Oso, with his machine pistol, enforced them; the ambassador, still dazed and in pain, did not work; Alicia and Sara, assisted by the old man, performed the light camp chores. That left Tono and me to do the more arduous work. We pumped up the two rafts, exhausting work in that heat, carried them to the river, and loaded them with supplies.

The big raft, a dull gray in color, was about eighteen feet long and six feet wide, with inside storage pockets, a small, manually operated pump for bailing, inflatable seats in bow and stern, and an aluminum frame secured to the air chambers on either side, with a small elevated seat in the center. The oarsman sat there amidships, looking downriver. The specifications and instructions had been stenciled on the side: it had been made in Idaho of two layers of rubber covered all around by a tightly woven fabric, and the air chambers were divided into four separate compartments so that if one, or even two, should be punctured, the others would keep the raft afloat. It was a tough-looking, virtually unsinkable little craft.

The bright yellow raft had been made in Taiwan. It was cheap and flimsy, something you might take out on a lake, but not down dangerous rapids. The cloth tag claimed that it had a six-man capacity, but there was just enough room inside for three men plus a little gear. There was no oarsman's seat; this raft would have to be paddled like a canoe.

I noticed that all of the essential supplies were being loaded into the larger, stronger raft. That made sense, and it also made me curious.

I asked Raoul which of us were going in the cheap boat.

"You, Tono, and my grandfather," he said.

I nodded. "Tono and I are expendable, but are you going to write off the old man?"

"I'm not writing off anyone."

"Grogan said that he studied the topographical maps and that there are some very bad rapids ahead."

"There are rapids," Raoul admitted.

"Bad ones."

"Not too bad at this time of year. We're still early in the rainy season."

"Who told you that? Dos Santos? Grogan said they were very dangerous."

"Grogan is a man who lies even when he believes he's telling the truth."

"Look, Raoul, your grandfather is too old to survive an accident in the river. Why don't you take him in the big boat and move Oso to the small one."

"No, Oso is big and strong. I need him to work the oars."

"The ambassador, then."

Raoul smiled and shook his head.

"Okay, Fox is a big investment. Alicia, then; she's young and I'm sure she can swim."

He shook his head again.

"Sara."

"No."

"Give the old man a chance."

"He will be all right."

"It was stupid of you to involve him in this."

"I know," he said. "I know. Everything has gone wrong, and something that begins so badly will probably end badly. But we can't turn back now. We simply must go where the momentum of our initial action carries us. We're just passengers now. You too, Racine."

"Grogan is certain that you'll be betrayed by Dos Santos. Dos Santos will get the money and we'll all be lost on the river."

Raoul shrugged. *"Puede ser,"* he said.

"Don't you care?"

"Not really. I'm hardly curious about the ending."

"I'm damned curious about the ending."

He smiled. "You can relax for today, Racine. We won't reach the Pongo Terminal until tomorrow sometime."

"What is the Pongo Terminal? I don't like the sound of it."

"It's a canyon, a gorge. The last of the rapids are there."

I asked, "Do you have any medical supplies?"

"Yes, quite a lot." He grinned. "Are you sick?"

"The ambassador is in great pain."

"I'll give him some morphine."

"And give him antibiotics, too."

"I gave him penicillin yesterday. I'll see that he continues to take it." He turned and started back toward the clearing.

"Raoul."

He stopped, turned back.

"Sooner or later you're going to have to do something about Comrade Oso."

"I need Oso."

"Maybe so, but the time may come when you'll have to kill him."

"Yes, and if that happens?"

"I'll do what I can to help."

He smiled wryly. "And you think I need help to pull a trigger?"

"Of course you do. You murder by proxy. Oso pulls the trigger for you."

He stared at me for a moment and then left.

Last night Oso had gone to the car with Dos Santos, the wax man, and Grogan, and he had returned with my suitcases. I went through them and picked out the items I would need for the raft trip: a pair of Levis, another pair of Levis that had been cut off into shorts, two long-sleeved shirts, a nylon windbreaker, sneakers and three pairs of socks, a wide-brimmed straw hat, and my shaving kit. Everything else would be left behind. I asked Fox if he wanted to take any of the clothes, since his golf outfit was not the ideal costume for a river journey through the rain forest, but he refused to reply or even look at me.

I was left alone at the river for brief periods while repacking the supplies in rubberized bags, and I managed to steal a few things for my personal survival kit: a half-dozen fishhooks of various sizes, a two-hundred-foot coil of six-pound-test monofilament line, three steel leaders, matches, a handful of salt, another handful of antimalarial tablets, and a packet of sewing needles and thread. I packed these things plus my passport, a small pocket knife I had bought in Las Playas Sureste, and all of my remaining money—one hundred and fifty dollars—into a waterproof bag. It made a fairly bulky package. I sealed the top, folded the package in half, stuck it down in my trousers over my hip, tightened the belt, and pulled my shirt tails loose to cover the bulge. It was not a very secure arrangement but it would have to do for now.

At eight o'clock I pushed the small yellow raft away from the river bank and clambered aboard. We drifted aimlessly for a moment, slowly revolving, until we left the back eddy and an edge of the current caught the raft and began pulling it downstream. The Indian, Tono, sat in the bow; the old man was in the middle; and I was in the stern where I could exert at least a little control over the direction and alignment of the raft. I didn't know anything about running rapids, but I had done some lake canoeing and I was certain that I could handle a paddle better than the other two, both of whom had admitted that they could not swim. I was captain of this lousy "ship."

The Indian and I paddled until we were in the middle of the river. The current was much stronger than I had expected; it hissed softly, like wind in trees, and the water's surface was corrugated into V-shaped waves and tiny whirlpools. Sunlight glanced off the water, shattered it into a billion dazzling facets.

Once into the main stream, Tono lay his paddle across his thighs and I used my paddle only to keep the raft bow-first. The raft moved about as fast as I walked when in a hurry. I dipped my hand into the water; it was surprisingly cold—melt water from the high Andes.

The other raft followed about fifty yards behind us. Oso sat above the others, looking downriver, clumsily levering the oars. He was strong, but it would take more than strength to bring that boat safely through the rapids. He did not have long to learn. Neither did I.

I tried, in my hesitant, ungrammatical Spanish, to instruct the Indian in technique. I explained that to control the raft properly in the rapids, we would have to move faster than the water or we'd broach, swing sideways, and probably capsize. We must dig our blades in deeply and paddle hard, with all of our strength, for as long as it was necessary.

"*Sabe, usted?*"

He said that he understood.

I told him that I would pick the route and be responsible for aligning the raft; all he had to think about was paddling, on the left side of the raft if I shouted "*izquierda,*" the right side when I yelled "*derecha.*"

"Do you understand?"

He nodded.

The old man said that if there were another paddle he could help us through the rapids.

"You just hang on," I told him.

He looked ill; his eyes were dull, old now, whereas when I had first met him up at his cave, they had been bright and alert. His face was paler then I remembered. There was no elasticity in his skin; it sagged, folded, blurred his features. He was dying here, away from his mountains.

"I'm sorry this happened to you," I said.

"I don't understand it," he said.

"It's hardly understandable."

"Kidnapping. Murder. Raoul and Sara? No. They were beautiful children, angels. There is something about this they can't tell me. If they could tell me I would understand."

I did not speak.

"There has been some mistake."

"You'll be back in your mountains soon," I said, knowing that it was impossible for several reasons.

"My dogs and goats—what will they do without me?"

"Your friends will care for them."

The rain forest was between fifty and seventy-five yards away from us on either side. The many different shades of green, from the palest yellow-green to green-black, all blended together at this distance into a uniform green wall. The highest trees all seemed to reach the same height except for some scattered giant palms which curved above the canopy and burst into tattered umbrellas. I saw herons and egrets. And once, as we rounded a curve in the river, I heard the soft explosion of thousands of wings and looked up to see a fluttering iridescent cloud of parakeets. The river, hissing, pulled us along.

Two hours after leaving camp we passed a solitary Indian who was fishing from the bow of his dugout canoe. He looked at us, fearfully it seemed to me, and then when he saw that we meant him no harm, he smiled and waved. Later, we floated by a small farm that had been hacked out of the forest; a few acres of corn and manioc, fruit trees, a stilted shack with a dried palm-frond roof. A dog raced along shore, barking at us, but we saw no people.

It was very hot in the sun; my face was shaded by the straw hat, but my exposed hands were burning, drawing taut. We would have to rig some sort of awning tomorrow.

The big raft remained about fifty yards behind us. I glanced back from time to time and saw that Oso was still practicing with the oars. He had improved, he was coordinating them now in various simple maneuvers; pushing downstream with both oars; then pulling hard, holding the raft motionless against the current; then pushing downstream with one oar while pulling with the other, spinning the raft; and then quickly reversing the procedure and spinning the other way. Each time I turned I could see the white crescent of his grin burning against the dark beard. I didn't know the precise definition of psychopath, but I figured that whatever it was, Oso belonged in the category. And I could understand why Raoul was dependent upon the man: Oso was strong, and completely fearless, and he was the only member of the group who was capable of decisive action. Oso wasn't a third-rate Hamlet like Raoul. He might be crazy, but he was competent, a good man to have along in a fight or on a river. I saw that, and I also saw that he might kill one or all of us out of some brutal whim.

We ate a light lunch on the raft, some fruit, bread, and cheese, a bottle of warm beer that smelled like skunk. The river curved into the trees, straightened, curved the other way.

At first I had been fascinated by the beauty and mystery of the country, but after five hours it became boring; it all looked the same, the endless chocolate-brown river and the green walls of forest. The humid greenhouse heat siphoned away all my interest and energy. I felt a lassitude that approached sickness. We saw nothing alive except birds, no more Indians, no deer or great cats drinking from the river, no caiman sunning on the muddy banks . . .

The old man dozed. Tono sharpened his machete on a whetstone.

"Don't stick that thing into the raft, for Christ's sake," I said.

He did not turn.

I realized that I had spoken in English. The heat, the gentle rocking monotony of motion dulled my mind—I was more asleep than awake.

I splashed some water on my face and arms. The chill was momentarily refreshing; then the heat, by contrast, seemed even more oppressive.

The sounds of the river gradually changed: there was a new humming, and beneath that, a kind of muted clatter like the clicking of balls in a billiard room. I cocked my head, listened. The current was stronger here. The humming noise changed pitch, began to throb. The river twisted off to the right.

"Tono," I said. "Get your paddle."

He looked back at me over his shoulder.

"*Un mal paso,*" I said.

He sheathed his machete and picked up the paddle.

I shook the old man. "Hold on," I said.

He twisted around and looked at me sleepily.

"Bad water ahead," I said. "Hold on tight."

The throbbing hum increased in volume, seemed to vibrate in the air. The river's chevron ripples were longer now and there were splashes of white water where they converged. The raft moved faster, began to skitter over the roughened surface. I could still hear the clicking-billiard-ball sound. It seemed to emanate below me, deep down in the river.

I looked back. Oso, managing the oars, was still grinning. The others did not appear so happy.

The throbbing hum had turned into a steady roar, like the crashing of surf heard from a distance. Six-inch waves slapped against the prow of the raft. The river curved to the left; our raft angled toward the right bank.

"*Izquierda!*" I called, and Tono and I dipped our paddles into the water and I guided the raft back toward the center of the river. I wanted to follow the most powerful current through the rapids, where there was likely to be a deep channel. Rocks worried me more than speed and waves.

We rounded the bend and ahead of us I could see a long stretch of brown-white spume. The air was misted and refracted into faint rainbows. The sound changed, began to resemble the reverberating rumble of thunder. And the clacking-billiard-ball sound was amplified. It suddenly occurred to me that the noise was caused by rocks and boulders being rolled along the bottom by the current, glancing off one another—a submarine avalanche of rocks.

The raft was moving very swiftly now. The river narrowed, the angle steepened; we were running downhill. The water just ahead was shattered into spray, cresting waves, crescents of reflected sunlight, roaring chutes of foam. We entered a series of four-foot-high waves, the raft's prow surging upward, falling, rising again, falling. Brown-white water foamed all around us. We passed between two great boulders and then shot down a steep twenty-foot chute and then up the glassy brown slope of a concave wave which curled whitely along the crest. For an instant I feared that we would not reach the top, that we would stall, drift back into the boiling water of the chute; but then we climbed the wave, just barely, poised there for a moment, ready to slide forward or back, and then with a sudden stomach-lifting rush we glided down the far side and into a group of five- and six-foot-high crossing waves which approached from every direction, merging and rising all around us, mushrooming, tumbling, crashing. I saw the dark bulk of submerged rocks, the glassy sheen of sharply curved water, bursts of foam the color of froth on cocoa.

A relatively smooth stretch, and then again we entered an area of concave waves, all of them cresting, beginning to curl, but never quite breaking. I breathed mist. The air sparkled with sunlit spray.

Another steep chute, a quick bumpy ride down the roaring water-walled tunnel, and then up and over the end wave, the raft airborne for an instant, canted to one side and then plunging bow first into a secondary wave. The raft curved in the center, flexed, and then straightened. A cold sheet of water swept the length of the boat, striking my face and chest. The whiplash motion catapulted me erect; the rush of water knocked me back down. The boat spun unguided down the rapids, tilting, dropping, spinning, and then it was calm again.

The raft was half-filled with water, we had nearly capsized during the last stretch, but we were safe now, and I didn't know whether I was exhilarated or terrified.

The old man snapped his fingers as if they were the end of a whip. He laughed and began bailing out the raft with an empty coffee can.

Tono turned and sullenly stared at me over his shoulder, as if I were responsible for the chaos we had just passed through.

And I thought: tomorrow we'll reach the bad rapids.

I looked back. The big raft was just now exiting the final stretch of white water. Oso, working the oars, had the boat correctly aligned, and he was still grinning. The crazy son of a bitch.

"I don't know," the old man said, laughing and bailing. "This is an angry river."

SEVENTEEN

We ran three more rapids that afternoon, each longer than the preceding (the last one seemed to go on forever; it was at least nine miles long from the beginning of white water to the end), but none were as wild and dangerous as the first. There were no really steep chutes, no "holes," no six-foot-high waves.

The raft was difficult to control, but Tono and I acquired enough knowledge to "read the river" and select a good line, and enough technique to guide the raft through bow first—not an insignificant accomplishment for the first day.

The old man seemed to regard running the rapids with a mixture of delight and terror, like a child on a roller coaster.

Oso had the advantage of following our route and seeing in advance the sort of difficulties to be encountered, but still he got into trouble; once I glanced back and saw that his raft had broached, then swung stern-to, and had gone through the remainder of the white water backwards. But the big raft was much heavier and more durable than ours; it was strong enough to survive a serious error by the oarsman.

Two miles below the last rapid the river curved to the right, beginning the lower hook of a gradual S-turn, and a large crescent of open beach had been formed at that point. It was about seventy feet long, thirty feet wide, composed of heavy grayish sand which sloped upward to the fringe of the forest. We landed there, unloaded the boats, and began setting up camp. It was still fairly early in the afternoon, not yet three-thirty, but we were all wet and tired and reluctant to face any more rapids today. And too, the sky was clouding up for the afternoon rains.

We erected the tents, strung the hammocks, built two fires, one for cooking and the other for drying out our clothes and sleeping bags.

Everyone worked except the ambassador, whose face was pale and drawn taut with pain; the old man, who was exhausted; and Oso, who did nothing more arduous than carry his machine pistol up and down the beach.

Raoul and I were staking out the tent guy lines.

"What is he doing?" I asked.

"Who? Oso?"

"Yes. Maybe he's waiting for the marines to hit the beach. Why don't you tell him to put that gun away?"

"You tell him," Raoul said.

"We're not going to run away. There's nowhere to run to out here."

He nodded and began pounding in a wooden stake with the haft of his machete.

"My only chance of survival is to remain with the rafts and supplies."

"That's true," Raoul said cheerfully.

"I'll tell you one thing," I said. "That Oso is probably the strongest man I've ever seen. He was working those oars all day. I couldn't have done it, and I'm in top condition."

"Well, he's been chewing coca leaves and lime since breakfast," Raoul said.

"Get me a few leaves for tomorrow," I said.

He nodded, smiling faintly.

"Can I see the topos of the next stretch of river?"

"Why do you want to see them? We're committed to the river. We'll be going through the canyon tomorrow and there are no serious rapids after that. Either we make it or we don't. The topos won't help us through, Racine. They'll just scare you." But he showed them to me.

There were four series of large-scale topographical maps, which showed the contours and elevations of the land and plotted the courses of all the rivers and their tributaries. The first series covered the Río Fuerte from Refugio through the Pongo Terminal; the second, from the deep gorge of the Terminal down to the confluence of the Fuerte and Loco rivers (the combined river remained named the Fuerte below that point); the third series of maps illustrated the stretch of river down to the confluence of the Amazon; and the fourth followed the Amazon east to the city of San Pedro de los Mártires on the Peru-Brazil border. I estimated that the river distance covered, from yesterday's camp to the Brazilian border, added up to about five hundred and seventy-five miles. It looked like a vast, completely empty stretch of country, but here and there on the maps I saw penciled notes: mission, rubber camp, hacienda, oil camp, small town (and, underlined three times, *military garrison),* more haciendas, another mission . . .

I studied the Pongo Terminal. According to my reading of the map, the river passed through a seven-mile-long, 1,300-foot-deep gorge. The river itself rapidly lost elevation during that distance: it didn't look as bad on the map as Grogan's description, "halfway between a pond and a waterfall," but it didn't look good, either. I didn't know, but I guessed that perhaps the steepness of the river was less important than the fact that its tremendous volume of water was forced between the narrow canyon walls—the same amount of water as above, but with less area in which to dissipate the power.

I folded the maps, inserted them in their plastic case, and returned them to Raoul.

"What do you think?" he asked. He was smiling, but I could see that he was interested in my opinion; he was anxious about the Terminal, too, despite his bold, romantic talk about being "hardly curious about the ending."

"I don't know," I said. "I'm afraid it may be like shooting a couple of twigs through a fire hose."

"While we're trying to hold on to the twigs?"

"Yeah."

"Men have run the Pongo Terminal before. Dos Santos told me that Indians have done it in balsa rafts."

"During the rainy season? In high water?"

"I don't know about that," he said. He showed me a queer smile, his upper lip drawn away as if he were showing his gums to the dentist.

The camp had been established and Sara and Alicia were just beginning to prepare the meal when a sudden wind hummed through the trees and spread what looked like frost over the river. And then it began raining, lightly at first, then furiously, and then it became a deluge. Silver rain pellets jumped four inches off the water's surface; rain rumbled and crackled in the treetops and the sound was amplified by the empty spaces below. The wind arced the hazy curtain of rain, bent it, and then the wind was gone and the rain drove straight down as hard and cold as hailstones. We dropped everything, divided, ran for the tents. We instinctively segregated ourselves: the captives—me, Fox, and Alicia—in the small tent; the captors and the neutral—the old man—in the big tent.

Rain drummed loudly against the taut nylon. The wind rose, hummed through the guy lines and snapped the walls, diminished. It was dim here, and despite the coldness of the rain, stifling. Our exhalations condensed into clear beads of water on the walls and ceiling. The tent fabric was illuminated by shuddering flashes of lightning, and the ensuing cracks of thunder seemed to originate in the earth rather than the sky.

The ambassador had slipped and fallen while running toward the tent, hurting his hand, and now he sat in a corner with his eyes tightly closed, his face contorted in agony. He held his injured hand aloft like a torch.

Alicia sat close to him, stroking his temple with her fingertips, her own eyes half-lidded in sympathy with his pain, her mouth formed into an O as she softly crooned sounds without meaning. They both had suffered, lost weight: but while Alicia was now more beautiful than before (with her fine, boldly sculpted bone structure apparent beneath the translucent skin, and her clear blue eyes enlarged and almost luminous), Fox had become repellently ugly. His face had thinned without revealing the underlying bones; it looked as though the flesh of his face was folding inward, collapsing, and there was no skull beneath to halt the process. The old man was older and sicker, he was dying, but he still looked like a dying man, not one who had been dead for days. That was it: Fox appeared to be dead and decaying while he still breathed.

"We'll have to change the dressing on your hand," I said.

They seemed not to hear me. Alicia stroked him and crooned. Fox, his eyes still tightly closed, breathed as though he had just sprinted one hundred yards.

"Ambassador?"

His eyelids fluttered; he sighed and was still again.

"Alicia," I said.

She looked at me.

"Does he have a fever?"

"Yes," she said. "Of course he has a fever."

"His hand may be infected."

"Certainly," she said, and she turned back to Fox.

"We have to change the dressing on his hand. And he needs more antibiotics. And more morphine for the pain."

She wiped the sweat from his cheeks and forehead with her palm. "God, what they've done to you!" she said gently. The ambassador's mouth curved downward at the corners and he made a sound halfway between a sigh and a groan.

The rain stopped after forty-five minutes and I went outside. The sun glowed behind the thinning clouds. Smoky mist twisted up from the beach, and the forest vegetation glistened wetly. I went into the forest to urinate. Another world there; pale spirals of mist, a reverberating silence punctuated by raindrops falling off the higher leaves, a great cavern suffused by a pale greenish light. And disorder: great tree trunks, tentacled roots, vines, creepers, moss, ferns, flowers smaller than a dime and bigger than the bell on a tuba. And silence. The forest absorbed all sound, swallowed sound. I realized that if I walked one hundred yards farther into the forest I might never find my way back.

I returned to the beach. Fox and Alicia had remained in their tent, but everyone else was outdoors now, using the last ninety minutes of daylight.

Oso was not carrying his machine pistol now—perhaps Raoul had talked to him. He strolled around the camp, rekindled fires, stroked his beard, looked slyly sideways at me and grinned.

Sara was kneeling by the cooking fire. Her hair was tangled into a round mass of feather-like clumps; there was soot on her cheeks, and her lips were swollen and slightly bluish.

"How are you doing?" I asked her.

She looked up at me sternly, fiercely. "Fine! How are *you* doing?"

"*Así así,*" I said.

"Get me some water."

I carried the two plastic buckets down to the river, tilted their mouths upstream, and let the current fill them. Oso, grinning widely, pelted me with pebbles as I walked back to the fire. I set the buckets on the ground and kneeled alongside Sara.

"Should I use water-purification tablets?" she asked.

"What kind do you have?"

"Halazone."

"No, iodine and chlorine don't work in the tropics. The water here is probably good—what is there to contaminate the river? But you can boil it to be safe."

A pebble struck my shoulder, bounced off into the fire. I could hear Oso, behind me, laughing.

"I'm tired," she said. "And so hot and wet and sweaty. How can you *do* anything in this climate?"

"It isn't easy."

"The humidity—my hair looks like a cabbage."

I smiled at her. "You look fine, Sara, with your cabbage hair and starving-child eyes and puffy blue lips."

A pebble struck me behind my ear; I flinched, but did not turn around.

"Go to hell," Sara said. She lightly brushed her lips with her fingertips, then touched her hair. "I'll bathe in the river," she said.

"Will you meet me tonight?"

"Where?"

"At the far end of the beach."

"No," she said. "I can't."

"Why not?"

"Well, maybe. What time?"

"Midnight."

"All right," she said.

A pebble bounced off my shoulder, arced, struck Sara's thigh and fell to the ground.

"What are all these damn *stones* doing?" she asked irritably.

I touched her arm—"Midnight," I said—and I got to my feet and turned. Oso was standing twenty feet away, grinning through his beard. His left hand was cupped, filled with pebbles. He had removed his shirt, and his torso—huge, hairy, as thick as it was broad, sheathed in fat—was shiny with sweat. He was six inches shorter than me but he outweighed me by forty pounds.

"*Qué tal, Jaime?*" he said, and he picked a stone from his left hand, tossed it, bounced it off my leg. I suspected that he had been aiming for my genitals. Oso spoke rarely, and I was always surprised to hear so high and flutey a voice emerging from that huge chest.

He threw another pebble at me; it hit my right knee.

Everyone was watching us now. Raoul did not have the courage to stop it.

Oso missed me with another pebble. "The tough *gringo* boxer," he said happily. "Do you think you can do to me what you did to Cesar Caceras?"

I watched him.

"Hey, let's box," he said. "Will you box with me, champion?"

"Okay," I said.

I removed my shirt and shoes and we walked together down the thick sand of the beach to an open area. The others silently followed us.

Now, there has always been a lot of barroom talk about what would happen if a good ring boxer fought bare-fisted with a gutsy, blood-toughened street brawler. Some people believe that the brawler would win. He might, just possibly, if it were a no-holds-barred sort of combat, a biting, kicking, kneeing, eye-gouging, bottle-swinging brawl in close quarters. He might win. Perhaps, but even so, I would have to bet my money on the professional. The pro boxer has spent the best part of his life perfecting certain uncommon skills. Fighting is his vocation. He's thrown millions of punches, into the light bag, the heavy bag, at his shadow, in the ring while sparring and in the ring during matches. He's learned a dozen different punches and can throw them individually or in combination. He has developed certain reflexes and honed them hair-trigger fine; the pro, if he's any good, should be able to slip your best shot and nail you five times before you can cover up. Just as the good big man will almost always defeat the good little man, the good professional will almost always defeat the good amateur. I was not worried about Oso. Everything was on my side: my physical condition, my years of training, speed and skill, reach—and I had room on the beach to move. Put us together in a closet and I might not be the one to walk out.

We stood about ten feet apart. Oso grinned at me. He was confident. His great, hairy chest sagged with fat. His balled fists were the size of grapefruits. He moved toward me heavily, his hands low, his eyes on my eyes. He was still grinning.

I assumed my normal boxing stance. I did not look at his eyes: eyes too easily lie. I mostly watched him from his hips down; his hips, knees, and especially his feet, would tell me all that I needed to know. His hands were in my field of vision, but I did not watch them; a man can feint with his hands, but he cannot feint with his lower body and still deliver an effective blow.

Oso's feet were squared. He couldn't jab from that stance, especially with his disadvantage in reach; he couldn't throw a hard right hand without tipping off the punch with his entire body; he couldn't aim a kick at my groin without first shifting his feet. He might be able to throw a good left hook from that stance, if I let him get too close, if I did not properly read the flex of his knees, if I did not constantly distract him with jabs.

He was cursing me softly, cheerfully. I threw two long jabs that struck his face with a wet, meaty sound. I stepped in, jabbed him again and then threw two short hooks, moved back. Oso shook his head and shoulders like a dog that has just come out of water. I stabbed him again with the jab and then quickly backed away to avoid his head-down rush. He wanted to wrestle now. I did not want to wrestle.

Oso shuffled toward me. He breathed like a man whose lungs were half-filled with fluids. I feinted with my left and he brought his hands up, then dropped them. His mouth was bleeding, there were red marks on his cheeks and forehead, and one eye was beginning to puff. I threw a long left jab, missed. He was backing me into the trees. I circled to my right until I once again had open space behind me. I feinted with my left again, and when Oso brought his hands up I hooked under them into his ribs and followed with a straight right to his forehead, which almost broke my hand. The knuckles on my left hand were skinned and burning; my right hand was numb. The son of a bitch was created to receive punishment; heavy bones beneath that fat, a walnut-sized brain that you could not concuss, a nervous system indifferent to pain. I stayed away from him, throwing a long useless left every now and then just to remind him that I had it.

He shuffled after me, grunting like a pig. He spat blood. His teeth, when he grinned at me, were pink with blood. I snapped his head back with another jab. His blood-flecked torso gleamed with sweat. His right eye was nearly swollen shut. I flicked a couple of jabs toward his good left eye. Blind the bastard and then cut him down like a tree. He seemed bewildered now. He had probably never lost a fight in his life and he was beginning to understand that he was losing this one.

I led with a right, a mistake, and at the same time he threw a big looping right that landed on my left temple. I backed away, evading his follow-up rush. My ears buzzed. There was no pain, but my ears buzzed and I could not see him as sharply as before. My mind was just a little foggy, as if I had just awakened.

I figured that he would try the right again and he did, and I stepped inside and threw a good four-punch combination, two short hard lefts under his rib cage, a right to the solar plexus and then a right uppercut to the jaw.

The shock of the last punch traveled up my wrist and forearm and elbow and upper arm into the shoulder socket. It was the kind of blow that can kill a man because of the effect on his spine—you can snap a neck vertebra. Oso was hurt, but he didn't go down; he grappled with me, staying close, holding on. I tried a couple of shots to his heart but I couldn't get any leverage. He was slick with sweat. He smelled like ammonia. I tried to slip away but he held onto me. I brought my right hand around his back and chopped at his kidney with the heel of my hand. He threw a knee that missed my groin but numbed my thigh. He sprayed blood-mist in my face. I pumped my left elbow into his midsection six or seven times. He had me in a bear-hug—an Oso-hug. I had difficulty breathing. There was no pain but I could not expand my chest to take in air. A red film formed over my eyes. Think. What is happening? He lifted his knee again, struck the same already-numbed thigh. What the hell? I repeatedly slammed the heel of my right hand against his ear. Then I abruptly lifted my own knee, caught him in the genitals: he hissed, spraying me with blood and a metallic breath-stink, and I pulled free.

His mouth foamed blood; there was blood matting his beard. I moved in and hit him three times, a rising left to straighten him, a left below his rib cage, and then a hard right to his heart. He doubled over and I circled to my right, so that his head, lowered, was in profile, and then I hit him as hard as I could along his jawline. He dropped to the sand and his body arched rigidly, and he suddenly relaxed and was unconscious. I could hear the blood in his throat as he tried to breathe. He coughed, blood sprayed from his lips. His eyes were open but the pupils had rolled up into his head. He choked, writhed frantically for a moment, and then, still unconscious, he instinctively rolled face down so that he would not drown on his own blood.

Everyone was watching me: Raoul, Sara, the old man, Tono. Fox and Alicia had come out of the tent.

I walked into the river, picked up a large, flat rock and walked back up the beach toward Oso.

He was sitting up now, coughing blood.

"No, Racine," Raoul said.

I raised the rock high over my head.

Raoul had drawn his pistol. "I'll kill you, Racine."

I did not believe that Raoul had the guts to kill me. But I wasn't sure. I threw the rock aside.

At midnight I left my hammock and walked to the far end of the beach. I waited for half an hour, attacked by gray clouds of gnats and mosquitoes, but Sara did not come.

I did not sleep very well. My ribs hurt, there was a lump on my temple, both of my hands hurt. I waited for Oso to come with his machine pistol and kill me.

EIGHTEEN

Once again I was awakened just before dawn by the shrill demented cacophony of the birds. I unzipped the mosquito netting on my hammock, climbed out, and walked barefoot down the rain-wet sand to the river. I moved slowly to avoid alarming the birds. I could still see the moon and a few late stars against the graying sky. It appeared that a glossy light was rising from the river rather than descending from the sky, crawling up the sloping beach and into the forest. No one else was awake; the tents were just shadowy pyramids against the dawn light. The river, broad and still moon-rippled, chattering and hissing, hurried toward the sea.

I sat on the sand with my back to the river. I did not move while light gradually infiltrated the air. The rain forest emerged, massive and overwhelming at first, terrifying, and then the various details appeared; barkless trunks like fluted marble columns, the most intricate of leaves, lacy ferns, ivy, creepers, palms, night flowers (closing now) and day flowers (opening)—vegetable life so profuse that I felt somehow diminished, though not unhappy.

I turned my head slowly, looking for the birds. There, a brilliant green macaw; a black and yellow toucan with a horny beak that looked like polished wood; a couple of insolent parrots; a large white rooster-tailed bird—a cockatoo? And hummingbirds, whirring rainbows. And up there, not birds at all, but a small colony of chattering monkeys that looked like emaciated, naked old men. They watched me fearfully, moving forward for a better look and then retreating in panic. Another bird, or primate, gave out prolonged ululating screams; I looked for it, but it was invisible in the brush.

Time swiftly unraveled; for an instant I became a component of the forest like the birds and monkeys and plants, and then I yawned and became the first true man, suddenly capable of wondering about myself and this strange planet, separate now—a nostalgic exile. I remembered something, or forgot something—the result is often the same.

I stood up. The forest took offense. Birds screeched, beat away into the shadows; the monkeys howled dismally, sounding betrayed, and then hysterically scrambled through the high branches of the trees, still, at last sight, looking like a group of nude, wizened but agile old men.

I got a few toilet articles from my kit, stripped to my shorts, and waded thigh-deep into the river. The water was cool; the current felt heavy against my legs.

I lathered myself with soap, ducked beneath the surface to rinse, lathered again, rinsed all the soap off except for my face, and then I went up the beach and shaved. Only Sara and I were making an effort to keep clean. Oso stank like a bear; Raoul, the ambassador, Tono, and the old man were beginning to resemble skid-row derelicts. Alicia occasionally combed her hair, but that was all. I thought it was a sign of low morale. Low morale, and we had only begun what was a difficult and dangerous journey.

I went back into the river and swam out thirty yards, until I was inside the strong current, and then I turned and stroked hard toward shore. The current swept me down the entire length of beach. As I waded up through the shallow water, I saw that Raoul had come out of the big tent and was standing quietly, watching me. He lit a cigarette and walked toward me.

"Aren't you afraid of piranhas?" he asked.

"I didn't think about them."

"What about anacondas, or poisonous snakes?"

"What about them?"

"You're a fool. There are dangerous animals in the forest."

I smiled. "Yes. But I'll tell you, Raoul. No fish has ever kidnapped me. No snake has ever prepared, twice, to execute me. A jaguar didn't bite off four of the ambassador's fingers. Do you understand what I'm telling you? Maybe I'm a fool, but I'm only frightened by some of my fellow higher animals."

He smiled faintly and nodded. "Just your fellow humans?" he asked mockingly. "Not bears?"

"Osos, yeah. And ideologues like you."

"Don't worry about Oso."

"You should not have prevented me from killing him."

"You are fairly dangerous yourself, my friend," he said lightly. "But there is no need to fear Oso after the fight. He respects you now. He doesn't fear you—Oso fears nothing—but he isn't contemptuous of you any-more. He admires your skill. I think he even likes you a little now."

We started walking along the beach.

"Raoul, I think we ought to scout the rapids before we enter them. We were lucky yesterday. Today let's beach the rafts and walk along the bank and select the best line through the white water."

He thought about it; shook his head. "It would take too long. You can see how thick the growth is along the river. It would take hours to cover just a mile or two."

"What's the hurry? Look, we can avoid the bad sections on the river that way. And if we can't avoid a certain pitch, we can portage the rafts and supplies around it."

"No," he said firmly. "Absolutely not. The big raft alone weighs three hundred and eighty pounds. How would we carry it through the forest?"

"Deflate it."

"No. We don't have the time. We have only enough supplies to last a week or so. No, Racine."

Raoul was beginning to enjoy authority, power, decisions. He was a natural follower who had somehow, almost accidentally, become a leader, and he liked the emotion. He was evolving: he was part-way between what he had been and what he was becoming. I had been able to partly influence the old Raoul, the arrogant embassy chauffeur; but the kidnapper-murderer could not be reached.

While breakfast was being cooked, I fashioned a crude life preserver for myself out of two of the medium-sized rubberized bags. I blew them two-thirds full of air, sealed and tied off the mouths, and then contrived a harness with my belt and a length of nylon line. One bag bulged out at my chest, another from my back. It was an awkward arrangement and probably not strong enough to last for more than a few minutes in the rapids, but a few minutes just might be the difference between living and dying. I asked the old man and Tono if they'd like me to fashion similar life preservers for them. The old man looked at me incredulously and shook his head. "I'd rather drown than wear one of those," he said. Tono was not interested, either.

Oso laughed at me. "Look at the woman with a tit in front and a tit in back," he said. It was definitely not macho to openly care about your life. One of Oso's eyes was black and swollen shut; there was a lump on his forehead, cuts, blood matted in his beard and dried blood on his puffy lips. He was not mean or sullen, as I'd expected; he seemed, as Raoul had said, to almost like me. I didn't know what that meant; perhaps that it might depress him slightly if he cut off my fingers or shot me.

I removed the life vest and tossed it into the back of the small raft, along with a packet of coca leaves that Raoul had given me.

I was halfway through breakfast—beans, rice, canned corned beef—when I realized that Fox and Alicia had not come out of their tent. I went to them.

The inside of the tent stank of sickness, sweat, the acetone odor of the exhalations of two persons who have not taken food in a long time, and the smell of rot—the infection in Fox's hand.

The ambassador was a sick man physically, but it seemed to me that both he and Alicia were becoming sick in another, more serious way. Their despair and withdrawal, their stubborn refusal to even attempt to adjust to the changes in their lives, hinted of madness. And each enforced the other in the flight from reality.

I moved further inside the tent. "Let me look at your hand," I said.

The ambassador kicked out at me. "Get away from me, you bastard!" he said.

"We've got to clean your hand and change the dressing."

"Don't come near me," he said, half threatening, half pleading. "Go back with your friends, you traitorous scum."

"Please," Alicia said. "Leave us alone, please."

"You two aren't going to make it," I said.

"We're together," she said. "Can't you see that?"

I had no reply for that. "You have ten or fifteen minutes, and then we'll have to take down the tent."

"Traitor!" the ambassador said. "You're collaborating with them."

"Try to remember," I told him, "that the good guys and the bad guys are mutually dependent for the time being. Oso murdered two of your friends, Ambassador, and he cut off your fingers. He's a stupid, brutal, dangerous man. But if you're alive this evening it will be because Oso brought your raft through the Pongo Terminal."

"You're in with them," Fox said scornfully, his eyes glistening with rage and fever. "You've been involved in this from the beginning. I told you, Alicia—he's one of them. The fight yesterday was just a falling-out of thieves. Now they're thick as thieves again. I told you, Alicia."

"I know, sweet, I know," she crooned softly.

Half an hour later we were on the river. We floated through the big S-turns and then the river straightened for a few miles. The water was half in sunlight, half in shadow. We stayed in the comparatively cool shadows. The sun rose higher, turned the trees an incandescent green, pushed the shadows off the river and into the forest. Sunlight blurred the humid air. My clothes were heavy with sweat. I had the feeling that I could not get quite enough oxygen. Far ahead, indistinct in the wavering heat blurs, I saw some low, forested hills and, beyond them, more hills that were high enough to be called mountains. Vultures spiraled upward in the thermal drafts above the hills. I saw a caiman, warty and open-jawed, sunning on the muddy bank to the west. And then, further on, more of them—fifty, a hundred, maybe more. Many had their jaws spread wide, as if greedily devouring the morning sunlight. We passed long-legged water birds—cranes, egrets, herons—picking through the mud flats. They moved jerkily, bobbing and weaving, their long necks coiling and then striking out like snakes. Some of the birds stood on one leg and spread their wings out like frazzled laundry to dry in the sun. For some reason the birds amused the old man; he pulled his straw hat farther down over his eyes, hunched his shoulders, and began silently laughing. His body quaked with laughter.

And then we rounded a curve and I saw the sunlight prismatically shattering on an avalanche of white water. So many of these rapids began just beyond a twist in the river. You were floating along, drowsy and weak from heat, and then suddenly the water erupted below, and it was too late to do anything but shoot on through.

"*Mal paso!*" the old man shouted happily.

It was furious water, but there were not many rocks and it was short; we were spilled out into the calm water below without having time to apply strategy or technique or strength. The force, the thundering brown-white rushing power of even a moderately difficult rapid, did not permit us to exert much control over the raft.

We had a smooth stretch of perhaps half a mile and then the river whitened again and slanted downhill in a series of steps: short rapid, smooth water, another rapid, smooth water, more rapids. The air throbbed. We dropped steeply, roller-coastering down the foamy waves, leveled, dropped again. The raft was half-filled with water. We scraped a rock, spun sideways, turned a three-hundred-and-sixty-degree revolution before entering the next calm. The Indian and I managed to realign the raft and take a moment's rest before entering the next rapid. The old man laughed and cursed and bailed.

And then we were finally out of it. I looked back: a roar like the ocean surf over a reef, sunlight splintering on the faceted waves, a mist like white wood-smoke. Nothing else, and then, like a craft plowing through a thick fog, the big raft loomed up behind us.

Far ahead, the river curved and entered a notch between two mountains. I could see the sheer rock walls of the canyon and hear, even at this distance, a persistent low drumming noise—snare drums, bongos, kettle-drums, bass drums. The air vibrated with a sound like thousands of drums.

"Oh, Jesus Christ," I said.

"*Mal paso!*" the old man shouted. He was so excited he beat his knees with his fists. He *liked* this form of suicide.

I thought of beaching the raft; we could rest, eat something, prepare the rafts and ourselves for the gorge. But I did not think any of us except the old man could tolerate the anxiety, and either eat or rest, while below us the Pongo Terminal drummed and smoked the air. It was best to get it over with.

The old man bailed. Tono, up in the prow, rested. I put on my improvised water wings, picked up a couple of the coca leaves and hurriedly began chewing. They were bitter. I swallowed the saliva and spit out the leaf pulp.

The muddy water was glazed white with sun and flowed swiftly downward. The hills rose on either side. The raft moved faster; the current made sounds like fabric being torn. And I could now once again hear the clatter of rocks rolling down along the bed of the river.

The big raft was about eighty feet behind us. Oso was eating something. Coca leaves.

Our raft was rocking in the waves. Close ahead I could see the sheer rocky V-shaped walls of the gorge. The river rumbled and chattered. Sunlight on the river hurt my eyes.

Now the waves were bigger, foaming along the crests. The white-tipped waves converged and funneled foamily between a pair of great boulders. We skimmed through. My lips were numbed from the coca leaves. I began chewing on some fresh leaves. My gums were numbing too, in the same way as when I'd had a shot of Novocaine at the dentist's. I clicked my teeth together; I could hear but not feel them strike.

The old man, still bailing, giggled and talked to himself.

Ahead, all around me, behind me now too, the river leaped into the air, fell back, lunged again.

I backwatered to bring the raft into line, and then I started stroking with my paddle. *"Izquierda!"* I shouted to Tono.

The air cracked, thundered, smoked. The water was exploding all around us, as if mines had been planted: waves swelled up, turned concave, burst, fell back, and rose up again. I inhaled rainbows. Water curved smoothly, glassily around submerged rocks and then seethed into brown-white froth. We tobogganed down a foaming avalanche, leaped up, airborne for an instant, slid downward. Spray whipped my face and chest. I could smell and taste the river. We were spinning down a long tunnel; I could see nothing but the rock walls on either side, the great waves, and a thin whirling strip of blue sky above. A flat facet of wall, white-painted letters: *Sal si puedes!* Get out of here if you can! What lunatic had come in here with paint and a brush to write that message on the rock?

And then the river suddenly dropped away beneath us and we plummeted down into a great funnel-shaped hole in the river. A whirlpool. And then we were turning, not too quickly, around and around the base of the hole with the slanted funnel walls revolving above us. The raft was canted at a sharp angle; centrifugal force pinned us there. I observed, almost dreamily, that the whirlpool was spinning rapidly clockwise, and concluded that we were south of the equator, otherwise . . . I looked up and saw a blue circle of sky. The raft rose halfway up the funnel, slid downward again—were we going to be swallowed by the vortex? Was there a vortex? I didn't see anything that looked—and now we were rising up the steep wall again, almost to the lip, and then we fell back. Could this thing hold us here for hours, days, weeks?

We hissed back up the wall, spun out over the lip, and were once again back into the motion and roar and confusion. The old man was gone. Perhaps we had lost him in the hole, maybe above—I didn't know. I just knew that he was gone now.

We were riding through chaos. The raft leaped and bucked, compressed, straightened. And now the Indian was gone. I saw his head for an instant, looking up at me out of the thick foam. I leaned out and offered my hand, but he was gone.

The raft spun away, tilting and rocking, standing on its bow and then its stern. The ten-foot waves crackled like newspapers being crumpled, and then they collapsed into spume. I was immersed in the heart of smoke and thunder. Rocks, cliff walls, water, sky, swiftly spun into blurs. Dazzling sun-bright drops of water hazed the air. Now a long downsliding chute, like dropping off the edge of the world, an upspewing explosion, down again. I hugged the floor of the raft. Was I shouting?

It went on. I gagged, vomited bile and river water. Falling, rising, spinning. My consciousness dimmed. I was a child. I was old. I was dead. Thunder cracked against my ears like fist-blows. I could take it. Couldn't I take it? I had been hit before. You simply held on and then hit back.

The raft has mysteriously vanished and I am tumbling through the cold water. Waves tower far above me. I rise, see an ocean of identical waves, fall down into the trough. Foam crashes around me, carries me down. I breathe foam. Drink it. Ride it. I am dying. Something strikes my legs. A submerged rock? Again, and once more, dull, heavy blows. I lift my legs and rush feet-first down the mushroom-bubbling cauldron.

Another heavy impact. No pain, but I do not know how badly I am being hurt—these blows might be killing me. Where is my raft? Where are my friends?

Ah, give it up. This will never end. Give it up, die. It just isn't worth it. All this turmoil—it just goes on and on, there isn't an end.

And I let go, I drifted down to greet death. Death was warmth and grayness and silence. Death embraced me.

"I'm so glad to see you," Death said tenderly. "Was it a difficult journey?"

"Yes," I said. "It was terrible. I tried to live but I became exhausted."

"Of course you did," Death said soothingly. "I know, I was watching; you were resolute."

"Where is the old man, and Tono?"

"They're here, don't worry."

"I'm not sure," I said.

Death hugged me tighter. "Please, it's all over now. Rest, rest."

"No!" I cried.

Death released me. "Well, of course, if that's what you want, truly. I can wait. But really, there isn't any point. Be honest—you did not like it up there very much anyway, did you?"

"But I think I can make it!"

"Try, then." Death kissed me on my cheek. "I'll see you soon enough."

I was drifting through the smooth water below the canyon. The air bag on my back had deflated but the one over my chest remained buoyant.

I choked, coughed violently, vomited. Below, the river gradually spread out into a huge, chocolate-brown lake. There were islands here and there, sandbars, half a dozen different channels. The current slowly turned me around. I looked back toward the V-exit of the gorge, and I saw the big raft rush down out of the mist-fogged air of the rapids.

They were looking for survivors. All I had to do was swim against the current for a few minutes and then splash the water and wave my arms.

Oso hauled me into the raft. "Here's an ugly fish," he said. "Look at him, all eyes and mouth. Shall we throw him back? Hey, what do you say, fish?"

I vomited river water into the bottom of the raft.

NINETEEN

We looked for the bodies of Tono and the old man for about an hour—Sara insisted that they be found and given a "decent burial." She could not bear the thought that her grandfather would be eaten by fish, caiman, crabs, eels . . . all the crawling and finning creatures of the river. And the birds, she said; what if he is washed up on a shore and the vultures eat him?

Oso, sweaty, his lips bleeding into his beard (perhaps he had reinjured his mouth in the rapids), a wad of coca leaves bulging in his cheek, rowed back and forth below the exit to the gorge, and then finally he shipped the oars and let the current take us.

"Raoul," Sara cried. "Stop him—we must keep looking."

The river seemed slower now than at any time during the journey. The big raft lazily revolved downstream, drifting among the islands and sandbars and uprooted floating trees. We were silent, and perhaps because of that we saw more game than before: more birds, flocks of long-legged, long-necked water birds; arrogant, brilliantly plumed macaws and toucans and parrots; hawks and eagles, kites; dementedly timid monkeys; a deer drinking water from the river; caiman scattered around the silt banks like rotten logs.

Perhaps the Pongo Terminal provided a barrier that kept out all but the boldest hunters and trappers. This felt like a true wilderness. It did not look much different than the river and rain forest above, but there was a new feeling, a significant hush perceptible beneath the usual sounds, as though time had been suspended here, outlawed, abolished—and the absence of time to urban man engenders an acute sense of dread. This jungle—and I thought of it as jungle now, not rain forest—seemed to me both alien and familiar. I had never seen nor experienced it: maybe I had dreamed it once.

Oso, exhausted at last, sat with his shoulders hunched and his head lowered. He applied the oars only once, when it was necessary to avoid a sharp, tangled tree root that looked like a squid.

The ambassador slept, or tried to sleep, or pretended to sleep. There were small sun-sores on his face. His white hair had turned faintly yellowish from sun and water. Alicia periodically dipped a handkerchief into the river and sponged Fox's neck and brow. She gave and gave and gave, infinitely generous: and he took and took and took, infinitely receptive.

Sara's face was grave. I saw her lips move, and once she made the sign of the cross.

Raoul, sitting alone in the stern, was cleaning and oiling all of the guns; Oso's machine pistol, his own revolver, a double-barreled shotgun, an old M-1. He looked up and saw me staring at him. "They're rusting," he said. He broke the action of the .38, fitted a clean patch of cloth to the cleaning rod, and then rammed it down the barrel. He was very intent on his work.

We floated downriver. The clouds gathered, lowered and darkened. It became like twilight. A fine rain, looking phosphorescent against the sky, slanted down and dimpled the water. There was a rich, heavy scent in the air: mud, decay, the living green forest, a metallic rain smell, and the not wholly unpleasant stink of the river— like earth and iron and wet fur and fish and electrical fires. Thunder drummed around the horizon. Lightning wrinkled the sky.

Oso began rowing toward a long, forested island which lay about half a mile downstream. Raoul packed the guns away in rubber-coated bags.

The rain suddenly came down hard, cooling the air and frothing the surface of the river. The island vanished. Rain fogged the air; rain came down so hard and swift that it was difficult to breathe. I inhaled through my cupped palms.

Oso was pushing the oars, grunting with the effort. Raoul cursed softly, persistently. Alicia, half standing in the raft, was trying to protect Fox from the slashing cold rain. Sara covered her face with her palms.

A shadow appeared to our right—the island. Oso adjusted the raft's angle, rowed hard across the current.

"Slow down," I said to him. "There may be sunken trees along shore."

His breathing was a rapid series of hisses and deep grunts. It looked as though the veins and tendons of his arms were going to burst through the skin.

"You might puncture the air chambers on a sunken tree!" I yelled over the sounds of wind and rain, and then I realized that I was speaking English to him.

There was no beach here; trees and brush grew right down to the river's edge. I grabbed the bow rope, jumped out into thigh-deep water, waded up the incline to solid land, and tied the end of the rope around a tree trunk.

While Oso hacked at the underbrush with a machete, Raoul, Sara and I unloaded all of the supplies and carried them a few yards into the forest. Fox and Alicia sat together on the muddy ground beneath a palm.

The roof of leaves broke the force of the rain; it clattered overhead and then descended from leaf to leaf, vine to vine, to the ground below. Occasionally the forest was illuminated by a vibrating glow of lightning, revealing the glossy greens and yellows, and then it became dusk again. Oso cleared enough space to erect the two tents.

The rain ceased as abruptly as it had begun. Wind tore ragged holes in the overcast and the sun glided into one of the openings. It was day again.

Raoul took out the guns and once again began cleaning and oiling them.

Oso spread a tarp on the muddy ground and lay down with his face exposed to a spear of sunlight.

The ambassador and Alicia remained beneath the palm; Fox shivered violently; his teeth clicked, and he groaned.

I examined my legs. They had been badly scraped and bruised by rocks in the Pongo Terminal's rapids.

"The flour has been ruined," Sara said. She had been going through the food supplies.

Raoul looked at her.

"Water," she said. "Rain, the river . . . mold."

"Is it all bad?"

"Almost all."

"What about the rice and the beans?"

"The beans are wet, and I can see some mold, but we can eat them."

"And the rice?"

"I can't find the rice," Sara said.

"The rice was in the small raft," I said.

Raoul looked at me. "What else was in your raft?"

"Some fruit, manioc, a few cans of meat. Not much."

"What else?"

"Three sleeping bags, two hammocks, Tono's machete."

"Did you have the fishing equipment in the small raft?"

"No, I don't remember seeing any."

"The fishing equipment is here," Sara said. "It's okay."

"Can you think of anything else we lost, Racine?" Raoul asked.

"*Two men!*" the ambassador said hoarsely.

"Sara, how much food do we have left?"

"The beans, sugar and coffee, salt, just a little flour that can be saved, lemons and limes, three cans of corned beef . . . "

"Christ!" Raoul said.

"You lost two human beings from the raft!" the ambassador said. His red-rimmed eyes were round; his face bristled with the salt-and-pepper beard, and was sunburned and dotted with raw sores the size of dimes.

"Yes," Raoul said. "Make a note of that, Sara."

The ambassador started to rise to his feet. Alicia tried to restrain him, but he shoved her away with his good arm and slowly stood erect. "Rice," he said. "Some fruit, manioc, a few cans of meat, three sleeping bags, two hammocks, Tono's machete, and *two human beings!*"

Oso lifted his head to watch.

Fox wavered. His clothes, filthy and wet and torn, looked two sizes too large. Golf clothes, net shirt, brown trousers, brown and white spiked golf shoes. He looked like a skid-row drunk haranguing passersby, but he might have been the sanest among us at this moment.

His voice was a gravelly monotone. "Rice, some fruit, manioc, a few cans of meat, three sleeping bags, two hammocks, Tono's machete, *Tono himself, and your grandfather!*"

No one spoke.

He stared at us one by one: Raoul, Oso, Sara, me, and then back to Raoul again. "My God. Oh, my God, what kind of people are you to discuss lost food when two men have died?"

And then Raoul, ashamed and perhaps a little intimidated by the ambassador's wrath, began a disconnected monologue of revolutionary rhetoric: capitalism, socialism, the exploitation of the poor and weak, blood miraculously converted into money on Wall Street, disease and poverty for the millions with obscene luxury for the few, racism, fascism, torture, military dictatorships, the CIA, bloody counterrevolutions launched against the Latin American people by the capitalist running dogs, the Bay of Pigs, the overthrow of the legitimate Allende regime, the millions bombed, napalmed, shot and maimed ("Dollar deaths, sir!") in Vietnam, Laos, Cambodia; strikebreakers ("Did you ever hear, sir, of the time in Colorado when the Rockefeller lackeys machine-gunned striking miners?"), tubercular children working ten hours a day for ten cents an hour in mills—

"But that was a long time ago!" the ambassador exclaimed, outraged.

"It was the same system," Raoul shouted, gaining confidence and moral fervor now. "In rain forests like these," he cried, waving his hand around, "maybe in this very forest, the Indians were enslaved and forced to gather rubber. They were beaten, starved, tortured, treated worse than flies, murdered for examples and murdered for sport—yes, for sport, Your Excellency. The deaths, the suffering . . . and why, for God's sake, why? So that your father would have tires for his auto, and so the *patrones* could build palaces and an opera house out of imported Italian marble."

"That was a long time ago," Fox said. "That was stopped."

"It was stopped," Raoul said, smiling. "Because the rubber market collapsed. So listen, Your Excellency, please don't discuss the deaths of Tono and my grandfather. Tono didn't die gathering rubber for you, he died fighting you. My grandfather died in an attempt to make this a better world for poor men like himself."

Fox stared at him incredulously. Alicia was standing at his side now.

And then the ambassador commenced his own rambling litany. Free enterprise, free will, each man at liberty to make of himself what he may, the highest standard of living in the world, free elections and free speech, the greatest nation the world has ever known, a Christian land of God and law . . .

Raoul was laughing.

Fox switched from the defense to the attack. Soviet slave-labor camps, the massacre of the Russian peasants, midnight arrests and three-A.M. executions, purges, Stalinism, the Hitler-Stalin pact ("A concord of devils."), despotism, fear, slavery, oppression. "Is that what you want for your people?"

"No," Alicia cried. "No, Raoul, that isn't what you want."

"Racine," the ambassador said contemptuously. "Haven't you anything to say for your country?"

"You aren't talking about my country," I said. "You're repeating slogans."

Raoul grinned.

"And you aren't talking about your people," I said to him. "You're reciting your catechism. I don't understand how the two of you can argue politics now. Look around you. Isn't this the most beautiful and terrible place you've ever seen? A plague on both your houses— I'm going fishing."

I got a cheap spinning rod and three lures from the pile of equipment and walked south through the forest. I found a little space in which to cast and I dropped the lure out among the riffles of the current. The water was muddy. I did not expect to catch any fish, but I wanted to get away from the camp and the people there. I thought how wonderful a trip like this would be in the company of people whom you liked and trusted.

I cast again, released the drag, and let the current take the lure downriver. The only genuinely simple people in the party, the old man and Tono, were dead. And me? A fisherman.

I heard noise behind me in the underbrush. I did not turn; I reeled in the line, wrist-whipped the fishing rod, and watched the lure arc out into the air and then drop into the water.

"Any luck?"

Sara: she moved beside me.

"No."

"Catch some fish. I don't care to eat just beans and bread tonight."

"Fishing isn't good in high, muddy water."

"Why are you fishing, then?"

"Why not?"

"Raoul says we'll have to live off the land and river for a few days, since we lost so much of the food."

"That isn't as easy as Raoul makes it sound."

She was silent as I wound in the line and cast again.

"Are they still arguing?" I asked.

"Yes. Fighting and drinking *aguardiente*. Oso found two bottles of *aguardiente* in a supply bag."

"He probably put them there. Is Fox drinking too?"

"Yes."

I unclipped the lure from the leader and attached another, a silver-and-red spoon. I could not picture Fox drinking and debating with Raoul, but it seemed a good sign; maybe he was finally coming out of his shell.

Sara remained with me for twenty minutes and then returned to camp. I fished until after dark, trying each of the lures without luck.

A small fire was burning in an open space between the two tents. Sara was baking small bread cakes in a tinfoil reflector oven.

Raoul and Oso were still drinking, but neither of them appeared drunk. The ambassador had fallen asleep on the ground. Alicia, his guardian angel, was watching over him. I kneeled on the ground and looked at his injured arm in the glow from the fire. His arm, above what remained of the filthy bandage, was swollen and inflamed.

"How much did he drink?" I asked.

"A lot," she said. "He drank for the pain."

"Why didn't he ask for morphine?"

"He is too proud to ask them for anything," she said.

"He drank their liquor."

I got out my pocketknife and carefully slit open the bandage.

"No!" Alicia said. "Leave him alone!"

"We've got to change the dressing," I said. "Now is a good time. Go get Raoul. Tell him I want his flashlight and the medical kit."

Parts of the bandage were stuck to the wounds and I had to tear them loose. Fox cried out, tried to turn away, but he was too drunk and fevered and exhausted to resist for long. He protested incoherently, writhed on the ground for a moment, and then with a deep moan he passed out again. His hand, wrist, and a part of his forearm were greatly swollen and blotchy with dark red and purplish blotches. The still-open wounds of his finger stubs oozed a white, stinking pus. His hand was rotting away.

Raoul, standing behind me, turned on the flashlight. "Jesus," he said.

"Oh, Gordon," Alicia said softly.

"What are you going to do, Racine?" Raoul asked.

"How much penicillin is left?"

"Quite a lot."

"We'll give him a hell of a dose then."

"Do you think that's a good idea? He drank a lot of aguardiente."

"Raoul, I don't think we ought to worry about mixing booze and antibiotics right now. His hand is rotting. Alicia, get me some clean bandages out of the kit."

"Aren't you going to clean his hand first?" Raoul asked.

"Why? To prevent infection?"

"Is it bad, Racine?"

"Of course it's bad. Look at it."

"How bad?"

"I'm not a doctor," I said. "Look at his hand. Is that blood poisoning, gangrene?—I don't know. But if it was my hand I'd ask Oso to get out his knife and cut it off just below the elbow."

"No," Alicia said. And then louder: "*No!*"

"How much morphine is left?" I asked Raoul.

"I don't know. Here, I'll see. Nine capsules."

"Are there any more coca leaves?"

"I think Oso has some."

"Okay, we'll save the coca leaves and the morphine. We may have to amputate this arm."

"No!" Alicia cried. It was almost a scream.

"Fox can decide tomorrow. If he agrees, then he'll need plenty of anesthetic, and something for afterwards. How much *aguardiente* is left?"

"About half a bottle."

"Christ, you guys had quite a party."

"His Excellency drank it down like mineral water."

"Maimer!" Alicia hissed at Raoul. Her face was bony, shadowed in the firelight. "Mudlator! Murderer!"

Raoul shook his head wearily and walked away. His back was straight, his head up; he still held his line.

TWENTY

The river had risen a few feet during the night and had turned previously dry ground into a swamp; small trees, weeds, and shrubbery rose up out of the muddy water and stirred faintly with the current. There was a vegetal stink in the air. The humidity was enervating: I had just awakened and yet I felt as though I had never slept.

I took the fishing rod and tackle box and walked several hundred yards to the pointed east end of the island. The brown river looked solid in the early light, like hard-glazed pottery or a lake of frozen mud. Below, other islands appeared out of the grayness as the sun lifted above the trees.

I cast and retrieved the artificial lures for about twenty minutes and then decided to try some sort of live bait—it didn't seem that any fish were going to take a lure in these mud-roiled waters. I turned over a rotten log. Insects and spiders scurried every which way; I saw beetles as big as mice, red ants, larvae, a pink spider. And I found some thick white grubs, put six of them into a tray of the tackle box, and impaled the seventh on a hook. Then I attached a lead sinker to the line, cast out beyond some riffles, and let the grub sink to the muddy bottom.

It was very hot. I still felt tired. Was I already beginning to deteriorate in this climate?

The sun scattered millions of needles of light over the river. I put on my sunglasses.

I felt a tremor transmitted up the line and down the length of the fishing rod and I jerked up the tip, setting the hook. The fish fought vigorously for ten or fifteen seconds and then suddenly quit. I reeled it in. It weighed about a pound and was a species of catfish, round-headed, black with a yellowish belly, scaleless and whiskered. It stiffened and quivered when I rapped its head against a tree trunk, and the luster left its eyes. I caught three more of the same kind of fish, then got out my knife and skinned, gutted, and filleted them.

I was about to return to camp when I heard the dull thunk-thunk-thunk of helicopter rotors. The noise grew louder, changed pitch. Birds cried out, flew confusedly from branch to branch. A flock of herons arose in a cloud and flapped across the river. They had almost reached the opposite bank when suddenly they panicked and broke formation, some continuing on to the far bank, others turning downriver, and a few swinging around and coming back toward the island.

Two big olive-green military helicopters appeared in the west. They were flying about one hundred feet above the water and a hundred and fifty feet off the island's shore. I might have hit one of them with a lucky stone throw. I could see the faces of men behind the windows and machine-gun barrels sticking out of the gun ports. I waded out into the water and waved my arms, but it was too late, they were gone.

I watched the helicopters as they chopped away downriver like a pair of great metallic dragonflies, and then they vanished behind a distance-hazed island. I could hear the clatter of their rotors for another minute and it was quiet again.

They were looking for us. Surely the ordinary river patrols, if they were such a thing, would not be conducted by two fully-manned military gunships. No, they were on our trail now. And they would probably find us sooner or later. Where could we go? Downriver. They would have spotted us today if our camp, for the first time, had not been established among the trees.

I met Oso halfway back to camp; he had been looking for me, and he was carrying his machine pistol.

Raoul, sitting cross-legged on the ground, was looking at the topographical maps when we came into camp.

"Did you see them, Racine?"

"The helicopters? Yes."

"What were they? The trees cut off a clear view."

"They were civilian—some oil company."

He grinned at me. "I saw them," he said.

"Then why did you ask me what they were?"

"Because I wanted to be entertained by your lie."

"Were you entertained?"

"Enormously," he said. "Do you think they are looking for us?"

"Do you want to be entertained some more?"

He nodded, smiling.

"No, they aren't looking for us."

"They know we're here on the river. I wonder how they know."

"Did you expect to vanish forever? The world has shrunk, Raoul—there's no place to hide anymore."

"Grogan," he said. "Maybe Grogan escaped."

"Or maybe Dos Santos got the ransom money and he knows he won't have to share it with you if you're dead or in jail."

"No," he said after a moment. "Dos Santos can't take a chance on having me captured. I could talk, you know."

Raoul stood up, folded the maps, and returned them to the plastic container. "We'll be in Peru soon."

"Do you think crossing a border will end it?"

"I hope you like raw fish, Racine. We're not going to build a fire. No more fires. And we'll be moving at night from now on."

"I love raw fish," I said.

I got a two-liter jar that had held instant coffee and squeezed it half full of lime and lemon juice. I cut the fish into chunks and added them to the marinade, put in a little salt, some chopped onion and tomato and bell pepper. Then I screwed the lid down tight and wedged the jar between two rocks in the river. The water was not as cold as upstream, but it still had a chill.

I did not see Fox and Alicia; they were probably inside the tent. Raoul and Oso were having a conference near the raft.

Some time after noon Sara prepared a lunch of beans left from last night and bread that she'd made from the last of the good flour. The fish had "cooked" in the citrus-juice marinade, but tasted foul; we ate the fish for the same reason we ate the beans and hard bread, because we were hungry and there was nothing else.

Alicia ended her fast; she came out of the tent to eat with us. She was becoming more ethereal every day; she'd lost more weight, was all bony arms and legs and huge, vague eyes.

"How is the ambassador?" I asked.

"Very sick," she said.

"Is he in pain?"

"Yes, yes, terrible pain."

"Did you tell him that it might be necessary to amputate his arm?"

"I tried to tell him."

"What did he say?"

She looked down at her plate. "He refused to discuss it."

"He refused?"

"He wouldn't let me talk about it."

"Did he understand?"

"Yes, he understood," she said.

She ate quickly and then started back to the tent.

"Alicia," I said. "Take him some food."

"Gordon can't eat. He just can't. He's tried and he gets nauseated and vomits."

She slipped beneath the tent fly, folded back the flap and mosquito netting, and went inside.

"That haughty bitch has been humbled," Raoul said.

"Shut up," Sara said.

"All of this has been worth it just to see her broken."

"If you can't pity them," Sara said softly, "then you can at least stop hating them."

Raoul raised his eyebrows. "What is this? Why, Sara, you can't change the rules of the game and talk about pity." He grinned and shook his head, looked at me, his audience. "My poor sister—a few days of hardship has given her the virtue of compassion. If she endures for two or three more days she might even attain sainthood." And then bitterness entered his mocking tone. "Sara, you taught me everything I know about hatred. No, it's much too late to change the rules of the game now."

It rained heavily for two hours in the afternoon. Soon afterward the river began to rise, edging toward the tents and gear. At five o'clock the helicopters came back upriver.

Clouds of gnats and mosquitoes arrived at dusk and we all took shelter inside the tents. I followed Raoul, Sara, and Oso into the big tent; I did not care to experience the air of demoralization and sickness in the small tent, Fox's and Alicia's obsessive suffering.

The mosquitoes were still there when we came out at night to break camp. They whined in my ears, got into my eyes and nostrils, bit and stung, drew blood everywhere on my body.

We did not completely escape insects on the river, though there were fewer of them over the water. I remembered that I had neglected to take the anti-malarial tablets.

It was silent except for the purr of the river and the squeak of an oarlock as Oso aligned the raft or pushed it back into midchannel. The river felt heavy beneath us; I sensed the enormous power. It was dark, we could see nothing, and then the moon rose above the ragged high edge of trees and scattered dimples and blurs of light over the water.

At false dawn we beached the raft, deflated it, and carried it and our supplies into the forest. The same helicopters came by two hours later, although Raoul calculated that we were in Peru now. "They're violating Peruvian airspace," Raoul said angrily. I laughed at him.

We ate some cold corned beef, slept, ate the last of the onions and tomatoes and peppers, slept, and then it was night and we floated the viscid, sour-smelling river. The Río Fuerte merged with the Amazon. It was huge, a moving ocean. Even so, that night seemed exactly like the previous night. And the next day's camp was the same as yesterday's.

Fox's arm became swollen above the elbow. The rotten pus-stink was always with us. He screamed if it was touched. Sometimes, on the raft, I heard him sobbing quietly. He refused to let us amputate his arm. We let him have the coca leaves and the rest of the morphine.

TWENTY-ONE

It was a few minutes after dawn and we were looking along the south bank of the river for a good campsite.

"What is that?" Sara asked.

"What?" Raoul said.

"Over there. No, farther down—do you see?"

"Probably a farm."

"No, Raoul, there are too many buildings. It must be a village."

"I don't think there are any villages on this part of the river."

I got the pair of cheap binoculars from a duffle bag and focused them.

A couple dozen dome-shaped, thatched native huts scattered around a big clearing in the forest; cultivated fields and orchards; a small house fashioned out of crudely adzed planks, and another long, wooden building with a large cross and a bell tower atop the steep roof.

"It's a mission," I said.

"Can you see any people, Racine?"

"No. Wait, yes, there are three—no, five—women down by the river. And some men standing near the church."

"Indians?"

"Yes."

"Are they looking toward us?"

"The women see us. One of them is waving."

"Damn it!" Raoul said.

"Why? What's wrong?" Sara asked.

"All of the missions out here in the bush have radio sets. And you know they've been alerted to watch for us. God*damn* it! We should have gone ashore while it was still dark."

I put the binoculars back in the duffle bag. "Raoul," I said. "Let's stop."

He stared at me from the stern of the raft.

"The ambassador is dying. We can leave him here. Maybe the missionary can radio for a helicopter airlift."

"You're crazy," he said.

"You won't do it?"

"Hell no, I won't. Fox is my future."

"More likely he's your past. Look, then at least stop and try to obtain some food and antibiotics from them. They must have some medicines there."

"Racine, I told you, they probably have a radio. Those helicopter gunships will be down on us within two hours."

"We're in Peru now," I said.

"I don't care what the nationality of gunships are," he said.

"Okay, look, we'll break the radio or take the crystals with us. Then the mission won't be able to send or receive. We've got to do something about Fox's infection. He's going to die."

He thought about it for a long time and then he surprised me: "Okay," he said. "You're right, Racine."

We beached the raft about two miles below the mission.

Ambassador Fox was more unconscious than asleep; he writhed, moaned softly and continually, and his eyelids fluttered but never completely opened. He smelled of death; his arm was already corrupt, his hand virtually deliquescent. The raw sores on his face had grown, were the size of quarters now, and the skin around them was sloughing away. They would be the size of half-dollars in a couple more days, and if he lived beyond that, all of the individual sores would merge and his whole face would then be composed of raw red new skin. But I did not think he could live more than a day or two without medical treatment.

Raoul: "Are you coming, Racine?"

"Okay," I said. "But I don't think you should wear your revolver."

"Everyone wears a gun out here in the bush."

"I don't think the missionaries will be armed."

"Come on, Racine, come on," he said impatiently. "This was your idea."

We left Oso, Sara, Fox, and Alicia with the raft.

There was a well-maintained path through the forest: The ground had been tamped hard and smooth with frequent use, and any interfering tree branches had been cleared away with machetes. I went first, Raoul followed a few yards behind me. I immediately began sweating. My limbs felt dead. Ten days ago I had been able to run up mountains, I had jogged at fifteen thousand feet, and now it was an effort to walk on flat ground at just a few hundred feet above sea level.

"We're an American film crew," Raoul said.

"What?"

"We're part of an American film crew. We're filming a documentary on Amazonia. The rest of our team is waiting for us at the raft. No, at the boat—we have a modern boat. But one of our men is sick with a bad infection. And we're low on food. Do you understand? We need medicine and we need food. And I want to use the radio transmitter."

"Okay," I said.

"I'm going to use the transmitter before I take the crystals."

I stopped and turned. "Why?"

"Dos Santos gave me a number to call in Brasilia where I could leave him a message. Maybe the missionary can put through a telephone patch."

"Do you really trust Dos Santos?"

"No, but I have to use him."

"I wouldn't have any use for a man who sent me down the Pongo Terminal and said it was going to be easy."

Raoul grinned. "I know."

"Raoul, Grogan was right about Dos Santos. He wants all of us dead."

"That may be true. But *he's* negotiating for the money. He either has the money now or he can arrange the exchange."

"Listen, if you were half-smart you'd forget the money and forget your comic-opera revolutionary organization. You'd drop Fox and Alicia off at this mission and then start running."

"It's too late for that."

"You want the money, don't you?"

"Of course I want the money."

I laughed. "And what about the poor and oppressed?"

He nodded slowly. "I'll have done something about that. Sara and I won't be poor and oppressed anymore. Now look, you're the leader of the film crew. I'm a cameraman."

"Do you know anything about photography?"

"As much as a missionary is likely to know."

"Let's go, then," I said.

"One more thing. If they are able to put through my telephone patch, I want to be left alone. You get them out of the way."

The path hooked inland for half a mile, then returned to the river before finally breaking through into a large clearing. Everything had looked neat and symmetrical through the binoculars, fifty acres of order imposed by man on slovenly nature; but it was not like that close up—mud, shabby huts, stunted crops and trees in the fields, chickens and pigs, a dirty broken-feathered eagle tethered to his perch, Indians who wore old-fashioned, poorly fitting hand-me-down Western-style clothes (probably donated by the faithful back in Europe or America), shy potbellied children, rusted tin cans, fish bones . . . The men spat and glanced at us sideways; the women, in separate groups, covered their mouths with their hands.

We walked past the chapel. It had been constructed out of green wood and the rough planks were warping; there were window frames, but no glass; a doorway, but no door; a bell tower without a bell. I glanced in through the door frame and saw a row of crude benches, a lectern, and a great plaster cross.

"And here the heathen savages sing hymns and are saved," Raoul said sardonically.

The house lay sixty feet beyond the church. It too was roughly built out of green wood, chinked with mud and grass, but there was a door and Plexiglas sheets tacked over the window frames. A small veranda, no more than ten feet by four feet, was enclosed by a heavy layer of mosquito netting. A man was standing on the veranda, his features blurred by the netting.

"Hello," I said.

Silence.

"We're with a film crew and one of our men is sick. If you could sell us some medicine and food . . . "

"Do you know any French, Racine?" Raoul asked. "Many of these missionaries are French or Belgian."

"I don't know French," I said.

"*Buenos días,*" Raoul said. "*Nosotros tenemos—*"

"Hello!" the man said loudly. "Welcome! I'm sorry—for a moment I feared you were the Judas scum from downriver." He had the voice of a stage actor.

Raoul stared at me for a moment, and then he felt his way along the mosquito netting until he found the opening.

"Come in," the man said. "I'll have my housekeeper put on a pot of tea."

We stepped through the netting and up onto the small veranda. He was a tall, very lean man with round shoulders and long arms and a neck that looked as if it had been broken and then set crookedly. His Adam's apple bobbed up and down as he talked.

"I have the wonderful Burmese tea that Millie liked so much," he said. "Please sit down, over there is fine . . . " But there was no place to sit on the veranda.

"Millie is in heaven now and so are the twins," he said. "They are stars now. How do you like your tea? I have sugar—we grow our own sugarcane here. How nice to see Caucasians again! I am Jacob Anderson."

His horn-rimmed glasses were secured by tape at the temples and bridge, and slanted askew on his face, so that one magnified eye appeared larger and higher than the other. He wore black city shoes without socks, and a wrinkled, frayed black suit.

He rubbed his palms together. "Well," he said. "You'll be attending the church services this morning, won't you. Yes. I intend to speak about Job."

"I'm very sorry," Raoul said. "But we can't stay long."

"Oh?" He looked angry at first, then embarrassed. "Are you Catholics?" he asked, looking down at his feet.

"No," Raoul said.

"Don't call me Father."

"We're members of a film crew," I said. "We've been making a documentary film of the river. Our boat is down below the mission."

"Oh, I can't permit you to film my Indians. No, no, they aren't ready. Come back in a year."

"A member of our party is very ill. He has an infection. We would like to buy some antibiotics from you, and morphine, if you have any."

"And food," Raoul added. "We're almost out of food."

"I don't have any medicines," he said.

"Could you spare some food?"

"Why, yes . . . although . . . "

"We'll be glad to pay you for it."

"I can provision you," the man said.

"And do you have a radio?" Raoul asked.

"Why, yes, I do have a radio."

"Could I use it? I'd like to put through a telephone patch to Brasilia. If you could contact a radio operator in Brasilia, he could telephone the number I want and—well, I'm sure you understand the procedure."

"I don't know. There are problems with that sort of thing."

"Could we try? I would appreciate it very much. It's an urgent situation—I simply must reach my friend in Brasilia."

"Well, we could certainly try," the man said cheerfully.

Raoul and Anderson went inside the house while I remained outside on the veranda. I was supposed to distract the missionary when Raoul had completed his connection, but I decided to hell with it—let Raoul deal with the situation.

"Here's your food," the man said, carrying a flour sack out onto the veranda.

"Thank you. Did my friend get his telephone patch?"

"Yes, it worked beautifully. There, sir, sit down over there. You look tired."

There was no more furniture on the veranda now than there had been the last time he'd invited me to sit down.

"The tea is nearly ready," he said.

We talked. He was mad in a gentle, sweet way. He and his wife, Millicent, and his twin sons, Daniel and Aaron, had come here four years ago from Missouri. His family was dead. Aaron had vanished one day, simply vanished off the face of the earth. Millie and Daniel had died in an airplane crash. They had become very sick and were being flown to the hospital in Iquitos when . . . well, there had been engine trouble. It had been G-G-G- . . . His will. Despite the terrible sacrifices and the hardship, he still found missionary work very rewarding. Although, it was true, the Indians were leaving him. They were going away one by one. After four years of sacrifice and hardship, they were losing their faith in G-G-G- . . . they were losing faith and returning to the forest to strip naked and paint their bodies and return to the old heathen ways. Oh, yes, and a few had gone off to the Catholic mission. But the fact was they were, one by one, renouncing J-J-J- . . . they were renouncing the Son of G-G-G- . . . the Son of Man.

"Oh, the Indians will come back. I've lost more than half of them, but some are still loyal and the rest will return. They have to. Millie and Aaron and Daniel have not perished for *nothing.*"

Still, he continued, it was possible that Aaron was still alive. He might have been captured by a wild Indian tribe, and someday . . .

Raoul came out onto the veranda. His pockets were bulging: the radio crystals. Anderson did not seem to notice; nor did he pay attention to Raoul's gun.

"We have to go now," I said.

Raoul took two twenty-dollar bills from his wallet. "A small donation to the mission," he said.

"Thank you so much. G-G-G- . . . " He shook his head in frustration. "Bless you."

We shook hands, I picked up the flour sack of food, and we left. We crossed the clearing and started down the forest path.

"Did you talk to Dos Santos?" I asked.

"No. I left a message for him to meet me in San Pedro de los Mártires in three days."

We stopped while Raoul threw the five radio crystals out into the river.

"He was a crazy bastard, wasn't he?" Raoul said.

"He's had a bad time."

"No one asked him to come here and impose his beliefs upon the Indians."

"I know."

"He could have stayed home in Texas."

"Missouri."

"It takes a hell of a lot of arrogance to come here and bully those people into accepting your version of G-G-G- . . . " He grinned at me.

TWENTY-TWO

Ambassador Fox was dead when we reached camp. It was very strange, Sara said. He had been slumped in the raft, groaning and shivering, when all at once he sat erect and stared around. He looked at the river, the trees, the sky, and then one by one at Alicia, Sara, and Oso. His eyes glowed feverishly, but Sara had the feeling that he was perfectly lucid during his last few minutes. He asked for water, drank almost a pint, and then demanded a pencil and a sheet of paper. He started writing and then suddenly stopped, lifted his head, and stared directly at Sara. She had not been able to read the expression in his eyes, she said: he might have looked at her with surprise, hatred, tenderness . . . anything. But probably, she said, he was not even thinking of her. And then he died. Like that, he died, hissing and seeming to grow small like a balloon losing its air. She showed us the sheet of paper. Fox had written just two words:

MY LAST

Fox's body still lay in the raft. Oso was digging a grave in the forest with his machete. Alicia stood a dozen yards away from us, looking out at the river.

I walked over to her. "I'm sorry," I said.

She nodded. She was very thin and her skin had acquired a translucent quality, so that I felt that if she turned her head just so, and the light struck her from a different angle, I would be able to see through her skin to the bones beneath.

"I know how you felt about him," I said.

Did she smile? She gazed serenely out at the river.

"You cared for him as well as any person could," I said.

"It's odd," she said. "When he was sick I loved him so much I thought it was going to tear me apart, kill me—my love. But now I just feel liberated. The instant he died I realized that I didn't love him at all, not really. It's very strange. I can see now that there was not much to him. Was there? No. What did I love so terribly, then?"

She waited for an answer.

"I don't know," I said.

"I was obsessed. But with what? Whom? Not Gordon. I realize now that I didn't even like him, not actually. I don't understand what happened to me. I think I must have been mentally ill during these days. I can hardly remember the days, it's all like an old dream, and all I have left is a feeling of sickness. *My* sickness, not Gordon's. And then he died *finally,* and I woke up. I feel freed, released. I want to laugh. I don't understand it at all. My God, I was committing psychic and physical suicide over that selfish, insensitive man."

She hesitated, brushed hair away from her eyes. "I was burning myself like incense at his altar."

"Yes," I said.

"And it wasn't enough. He wanted me to burn brighter, burn hotter, burn faster. I was consuming myself and he thought it was something I owed him. I felt guilty because it was not my arm that was rotting. I wanted it to be my arm. And Gordon wanted it to be *my* arm."

"How do you feel now?"

"I'm hungry," she said. "I'm thirsty, and I'm tired. I feel fine."

"Alive," I said.

She nodded and smiled faintly. "Funny. I see it now—he's the kind of man I've picked all my life. But I've never been able to see it because my relationships were never pushed to the extreme. My neurosis grew like a mushroom under all of this stress. Well, I've learned something. I learned more about myself in these few days than I would have in ten years of analysis. I saw myself and I'm frightened by it. I ain't gonna be a sickie no more."

She grinned, and then she started crying and the grin twisted.

"Are you okay?"

"Listen—I'm going to be just fine."

Oso struck water three feet down in the hole. We carried Fox from the raft, wrapped him in a tarp, lowered him into the grave, and then covered him with dirt. We awkwardly stood around the grave.

"Would anybody like to say anything?" Raoul asked.

We were silent.

"Racine?"

"No. I can't think of anything. But maybe Oso would like to tell us a parable about the relationship between the parts and the whole, the fingers and the man."

"Ask him, Racine. Your Spanish is adequate."

Raoul looked at Alicia.

She slowly shook her head.

"Sara?"

"I'm sorry," Sara said to the grave. "Truly I'm sorry."

Raoul stared at his sister for a moment, and then, with an irony that approached self-contempt, he said: "Your sacrifice has not been in vain, Your Excellency. You have contributed to the happy socialist future."

We returned to the river and opened the flour sack the missionary had given to us. We were all very hungry. The sack contained manioc, plantains, hearts of palm, maize, and some woody white roots shaped like carrots. Everything was more than half spoiled; we ate what we could and threw the rest into the river.

"Forty dollars for the missionary's garbage," Raoul said bitterly. "I'm glad we didn't have to rely on his Christian charity."

Oso had erected the tents while we had been at the mission. Now Alicia went alone into the small tent; Raoul, Oso, and Sara into the other. I was not tired.

That is, my body was fatigued but my mind remained alert. I sat by the water for an hour or so. There was considerable daytime river traffic since we had reached the Amazon: small diesel launches, barges, sailing rafts made of balsa wood, dugouts, ancient paddlewheel steamers, and occasionally modern freighters and tourist cruise ships running the twenty-five hundred miles from the Atlantic to Iquitos.

The river was high, growing higher every day, but the currents were not fast. I saw great trees floating along, masses of garbage that had been discharged from the ships, and floating islands. The rising water undermined the river banks, cut inland, and loosened great slabs of earth. Some were two or three acres in size, still thickly overgrown with trees and grass and shrubbery. The intricate root systems held the soil together in a mass and provided buoyancy. They gradually melted as they traveled downriver, and ultimately they would completely dissolve; but for now they were floating islands.

I slept in my hammock for several hours, got up after noon and broke open a rotten log for grubs, then went fishing. I did not catch anything. I slept until dusk.

We floated the river all during the night. It rained and afterward we were cold; the temperature did not drop below sixty degrees but it seemed like winter to us. The next morning I caught an eight-pound catfish and we roasted it on a spit and ate it with the last of the beans. Raoul permitted us to have a fire, although we would continue to travel at night.

It rained again the following night. I trolled a lure from the stern of the raft and did not catch any fish. After we established camp at dawn I went out into the forest, climbed trees, and looted bird nests of eggs. I collected forty eggs of various sizes and colors. We fried and ate the good ones.

At 4:30 A.M. on the third night we saw lights reflected off the clouds.

"San Pedro de los Mártires," Raoul said.

We beached the raft a few miles above the city. After the tents were erected and the others had gone inside them, I walked down to the water's edge to wait for dawn. There were not many mosquitoes around at this hour. The moon was down and the river moved darkly, heavily past. I saw the lights of a ship out in midchannel and heard the piston-thumping engines.

Raoul came out of the big tent and stood next to me. The orange coal of his cigarette flashed as he inhaled.

"Well, it's almost over," he said.

"Almost."

"It is going to work after all," he said. "At least partly—we still have Alicia, and I'm sure that Dos Santos has concluded the negotiations with her family by now."

"No, it isn't going to work, Raoul. It blew up a long time ago. You gambled and lost on a long shot, but you were too greedy to accept the loss and get out of the game. You lost when you had Oso kill Brecht and Datone, you lost when your three friends were captured, you lost when your grandfather and Tono and the ambassador died, and you lost again—really lost—when you brought Dos Santos into it. Dos Santos devours babies like you every day of the week for breakfast."

"I don't think he's that tough."

"He's not tough, he's smooth and smart. Oso could break him in half. So could you, probably. But he isn't the kind of man to wrestle with you. He'll just have you killed tomorrow or in a year."

"So you think he'll assassinate me."

"No, I didn't say that. Important persons are assassinated, punks are murdered."

Raoul laughed softly. "The results are similar." He inhaled from his cigarette and flipped it out into the darkness.

"When are you going to meet him?" I asked.

"Tomorrow."

"What time?"

"I said that I would stand out in front of the main post office building in San Pedro at noon tomorrow and every two hours after that until six. If we miss each other today, then I will keep the same schedule tomorrow."

"How long have you planned to meet Dos Santos here?"

"Since I contacted him and he suggested that we escape by river."

"You babe. Why San Pedro de los Mártires?"

"A small tributary river runs south at San Pedro and divides Peru and Brazil. San Pedro is on the Peru side of the river, and there is a town called Porto Pedro on the other side. It's easy to move back and forth between the two countries by boat or the bridges. As you can imagine, it's almost impossible to control the traffic along these wilderness borders—no one even tries very hard."

"So Dos Santos can slip back and forth between his own country and this one without much difficulty."

"That's right."

"He could, say, commit a crime in Peru and not much later be safe in Brazil. I've never heard of anyone being extradited from Brazil. Raoul, you are an idiot."

"I'm not as stupid and careless as you think, Racine. I will insist that Dos Santos come alone to make the exchange, and I'll make certain that we're not followed. And remember that I have Oso. It may be that Dos Santos devours babies like me for breakfast every day. But do you think he can chew and swallow Señor Oso?"

The light was coming now; trees, the river, blue sky had imperceptibly emerged out of the darkness.

"You've been a good boy, Racine," Raoul said. "Stay a good boy for another day and everything will be fine."

"Sure," I said. "I can be a good boy for one more day."

When Raoul had gone I went through the supplies until I found the small hand compass.

TWENTY-THREE

I dreamed that I was alone in the rapids of the Pongo Terminal. Tono and the old man were gone. The raft rocked violently through the huge waves and I dreaded the moment, coming soon, when I would be hurled into the river.

I awoke. Oso, grinning, was swinging my hammock back and forth. He released it when he saw that my eyes were open. His breath smelled like sulphur.

"Good morning, Señor Bear," I said.

The hammock gradually lost motion.

"Good morning, Mr. Champion."

Oso walked a few yards away. He innocently, almost modestly, glanced at me out of the corners of his eyes and then turned. He had the same bemused smile and the same glitter in his eyes as the time when he'd thrown pebbles at me. Oso courted the victims of his violence in the same way a shy adolescent might court the prettiest girl in his class. Now he cocked his head again, his eyes briefly flirted with mine, and he casually strolled off toward the eastern edge of the clearing. He had his machine pistol.

I got out of the hammock. We had camped in a fairly large clearing. It was close to the city, and many others had camped here in the past: there were fire-blackened stones, tin cans and bottles and refuse scattered around, and machetes had scarred the surrounding trees.

Oso was at the end of the clearing now, staring beatifically at a large orange-and-black butterfly. He smacked his lips, sending sweet wet kisses up to the fluttering butterfly, and then he glanced sideways at me and grinned.

I looked around the camp; Sara was sitting down by the river, but I did not see Raoul or Alicia.

The river, a muddy brown expanse feathered by currents and wind, was so wide here that the opposite shore was just a smudge on the horizon. A rusty old freighter was passing by several hundred yards out in the river; I could hear the thrumming of her diesels and see the sharp prow entry shear off continual, foaming waves which smoothed, rounded, and then rolled on an angle toward shore.

I walked down to the water's edge and sat alongside Sara.

"Where is Alicia?" I asked.

"In her tent."

"And Raoul?"

"He walked into the city to meet Dos Santos."

I looked at my watch: it was twelve-ten. "What time did he leave, Sara?"

"About an hour ago."

"It's only three miles—he made the noon meeting. Do you know why he went into the city?"

"Just to meet Dos Santos."

"Sara, he's setting up the exchange. He's going to give Alicia to Dos Santos."

She looked at me gravely. Sara had softened since the death of her grandfather; and softened more since Fox had been buried. The hard glitter was gone from her eyes now, and when she smiled it was not the same ferocious teeth-locked grin.

"Sara," I said. "This has to stop now."

"Yes," she said quietly.

"It's all over. Alicia must be freed."

"Yes. You are right."

The freighter's bow wave rolled swiftly toward us, swelled and turned concave as it reached shallow water, blossomed into foam, and crashed against the shore.

"We have to get away soon," I said.

"Oso," she said. "Raoul told Oso to watch you very carefully, and to kill you if necessary. There—look at him! He wants to kill you."

"I'll find a way to deal with Oso. But you must go with Alicia."

"No. I'll stay here."

"You must leave."

"What's the point? I would rather die than go to jail. And Raoul—he really isn't strong, you know. At night in the tent he sweats and whimpers in his dreams. Raoul won't be able to take what they'll do to him in jail. I have to stay with him."

"Listen, Sara, you don't have to go to jail. I have money in the States. I can have it sent down here. Brazil is just a few miles away, you can hide there. Christ, Brazil is a huge country, anyone can get lost back here in the river and savannah towns. With a little money you can live quietly for five or six months, and then when things have cooled, you can move on."

She smiled and slowly shook her head.

"You can buy a fake passport and fly, say, to Mexico—they wouldn't examine your papers too carefully. And from there, if you liked, you could easily cross the border into the States. We could even get married—just for a couple of months, long enough for you to get legal status in the country. The U.S. is filled with illegal aliens, one more won't hurt. I'll help you."

"Why?"

"It sounds very difficult, but it isn't, not really. You can live quietly, and then when the time is right you can move through any of these Latin countries without attracting suspicion."

She was smiling faintly. "Yes, yes, but why do you want to help me?"

"I don't know. Maybe because you started out to be the coldest and hardest of us all, and now you're the only one who seems to feel anything. Christ, I don't know. I'm sick of seeing people die. I don't want to see you die or go to jail."

She touched my hand. "Thank you."

"Don't just quit."

"Thank you, but I have to stay with Raoul."

"Why? Because he's your brother? He got you into this filthy mess."

"No, Raoul would have been happy to drive the embassy Cadillac all his life and go to the stadium to watch sports and drink with his friends and count his conquests—I guided him into this. You see, I am really the one who is responsible. It could not have happened without me. I changed Raoul slowly, I twisted him to grow in a different direction, as you'd guide a plant's growth. We planned this together, we recruited the others. I did it through Raoul. Our three friends in the jails of Quitasol, the major and the captain, my grandfather, Ambassador Fox, Grogan, Alicia, you. And think of the families, the suffering . . . "

"That's past, it doesn't matter now."

"Please," she said. "Don't tell me that it doesn't matter. If it doesn't matter then I've done nothing wrong. I have done wrong, I have, and if you take that away from me then I haven't got anything. I haven't even got remorse. Or death."

I got up and walked toward the small tent. Oso, still at the far end of the clearing, grinned at me, a slash of white against the blackness of his beard. His thick eyebrows were raised. He was tendering me an invitation. I declined.

I entered the tent. Alicia, sitting cross-legged on the floor, was combing her hair.

"You have to escape," I said.

She looked up at me.

"Raoul is going to give you to Dos Santos."

She slowly lowered the comb.

"I'm going to distract Oso. As soon as you see your chance I want you to walk directly back into the forest. Walk—if you hurry you'll attract his attention. Just stroll back into the trees. Do you understand?"

She nodded.

"Here." I got the compass out of my pocket and gave it to her. "Do you know how to read one of these?"

"No," she said.

I knelt on the tent floor, opened the lid, and released the needle. It swung back and forth, gradually decreasing in arc, and then settled. "The needle is pointing to magnetic north," I said, "not true north, but you don't have to worry about that variation, a rough reckoning will be good enough. Line the needle point to the N on the dial. You see? As soon as you get into the forest, walk south for a couple of miles, then turn and walk east. You'll come to a river. Follow the river *north* to San Pedro de los Mártires. There probably won't be an American consulate there. Go immediately to the police. Now repeat my directions."

"Walk south in the jungle for about two miles, turn east for three miles, follow a river north into the city."

"That's right. The first step is to get the hell away from here." I revolved the compass, locked the needle, closed the cover and gave it to her. "Show me."

She tried it.

"Let the needle float freely."

She altered the angle and then carefully rotated the compass until the needle pointed north.

"Okay. Once you get away from here, slow down, take your time. You have about eight hours of light remaining. It's going to be a long walk through very rough country, about seven miles altogether. Read the compass often, take your bearings."

She was very pale.

I smiled at her. "Hey, don't be scared. Any girl scout could do this. A cheerleader won't have any trouble. You can't get lost if you concentrate and refuse to panic. Rely on the compass. Don't start thinking that the compass is wrong and that you should trust your sense of direction. Use the compass. You'll be all right."

She smiled hesitantly.

"Don't worry about beasties," I said. "If you remain calm, if you watch where you're going, this little walk isn't any more dangerous than a stroll in the Carolina woods. There are copperheads and rattlers and water moccasin back home, aren't there? Of course. Don't let all these exotic-looking vegetables scare you."

"Okay," she said.

"You'll be fine. I'm going out of the tent now. Wait a few minutes and then you come out. Walk around the clearing, wash your face in the river, drink some water, anything. And watch. When you see your opportunity, go. All right?"

"Yes," she said. "Thank you."

"I'll come and see you in the States. We'll eat quail and drink bourbon and tell Huck Finn river stories."

"Jim," she said. "Good luck."

"One more thing."

She waited.

"Sara may go with you. Will you help her?"

"I think she'll be more help to me than I will to her."

"I mean, will you help her afterwards?"

"How?"

"Lie for her. Help her squeeze out of this mess."

She hesitated.

"There is no reason why you should help her," I said.

"It isn't—I don't want vengeance," she said.

"What do you want?"

"I don't know. Justice."

"Justice? How nice. I hope Santa brings you some."

I went back outside into the bright sunlight. Oso was still at the far end of the clearing; I think he hoped that I would run. Sara had not moved from the river's edge. It was 12:33.

I sat down on the sand. "I want you to go with Alicia," I said.

She shook her head. "I told you, I have to stay here."

"Now, listen to me, Sara."

"I have to stay with—"

"I said *listen!* Your remorse and self-pity isn't going to help anyone. Alicia needs your help. She's going to go into the forest, she's going to try to escape, but I don't think she can make it alone. She'll panic, she'll get lost. I want you to go with her. You *owe* her that. It's pretty much up to you now whether she lives or dies. Do you understand? The hell with your guilt. You claim responsibility for all of this. I doubt that's so—but if it is so, you can by God *keep* the responsibility now and go with her. Help her make it."

She stared out at the river.

"Okay," I said. "Then why don't you just kill her yourself. Borrow Oso's gun and kill her that way."

She slowly exhaled. "All right," she said.

"Kill yourself later."

"I said *all right!*"

"Do you know how to use a compass?"

"Yes."

"All you have to do is go south into the forest, east to a small river, and then follow the river down to San Pedro de los Mártires."

"I understand," she said.

I got out my "survival kit," unwrapped it, and withdrew the one hundred and fifty dollars from my wallet. "Here. This will keep you for a little while."

She accepted the money.

"Now, remember this name and address: Nacho Carmona, Aldama *novente nueve,* Bogotá, Colombia. He has a phone but I can't recall the number. Nacho's in Quitasol now, at the Hotel Cristóbal Colón. Now, if you need money or help, or if you want to reach me, contact Nacho."

Alicia came out of the tent and walked stiff-legged down to the raft. She was very frightened. She got a bottle of water from the raft and drank from it.

"Talk," Sara said. "Oso is watching us."

Alicia turned toward us with a bright, completely artificial smile. "My," she said, "isn't it a lovely day?"

Sara smiled. "It surely is, Scarlet."

I got to my feet. "I'll go tease the bear. Take off as soon as I get him turned around, but don't run."

Oso watched me approach as though he expected me to tell him an absolutely hilarious joke.

I stopped ten feet away. "Come on, Oso. I'll teach you how to box."

He grinned and waggled the muzzle of his machine pistol, saying no.

"I won't hurt you," I said contemptuously.

"You are very fast," he said.

"We'll just spar for a while."

"Are you fast enough to catch a bullet in your teeth?"

"Look," I said. "Left foot forward, right foot back. Shorten the distance you have to throw your left. Hands high, like this. You see?" I began moving to my left. "Move," I said, "shoot out the jab. Nothing breaks concentration or lowers resolve like a good left hand. Rip it in there, Oso." I threw a pair of jabs, hooked with my left, and followed with a straight right. I danced to my left again, feinting, ducking, picking off punches with my wrists and forearms. My back was to the river now; I had him halfway turned around.

"Combinations," I said. "Amateurs want to finish it with one punch. No, Oso, combinations, *series* of punches. And don't be a head-hunter, work on the body." I threw some short, vicious body punches at my invisible opponent. "And move, Oso. You know where you're going, but he doesn't. Move back, forward, to the sides, retreat and move in." I jabbed twice from long range, circled. Oso was facing away from the tents now. Beyond him I saw Sara and Alicia slowly walk across the clearing.

Oso was beginning to grow a little bored with my performance.

My adversary caught me with a tremendous blow that knocked me down.

Oso grinned down at me. He liked it better when I was losing.

I drew myself up on one knee and waited for the eight-count, and then I unsteadily rose to my feet. Sara and Alicia were into the forest now.

I defended myself against a barrage of lefts and rights, taking most of the imaginary blows on my gloves and arms, weaving and ducking. I was in trouble. I snapped my head to one side, fell loosely to my knees, and then toppled forward onto my chest.

Oso was laughing.

I had the heart of a lion. I painfully struggled to my hands and knees. Oso was still laughing when he clubbed me on the forehead with the butt of his machine pistol.

TWENTY-FOUR

It is a serious thing to be knocked unconscious by a blow to the head. Doctors will advise that you spend at least twenty-four hours under observation in a hospital. A concussion can cause intercranial bleeding. Often the hemorrhages in the brain are small and will seal by themselves; but sometimes they are large and continue to bleed, and a neurosurgeon must drill a small hole in your skull to release the pressure of blood and cerebralspinal fluid.

I do not know how long I was unconscious—probably no more than three or four minutes. It seemed longer, of course; a sudden unsought sleep is a terrifying experience, as disorienting in itself as the physical shock which caused it. I was nothing in darkness, and then I was dimly aware of being a thing crawling crabwise away from the confusion and pain. Dazzling light, heat, a salty-sweet taste, a gritty substance in my teeth, pain, sounds which seemed to arrive from a great distance. I felt that I had traveled to a far place, remained there for a very long time, and had finally returned "home" to find everything strange, not at all as I remembered.

My mind and body gradually reunited. Blood in my mouth and throat—a familiar enough taste. Sand in my teeth. Pain. The hissing of the river, wind, Oso laughing loudly. Oso was the kind of man who laughed at his own jokes. He smashed you in the forehead with the steel-framed butt of his gun for a joke, and then had to laugh all by himself because he had eliminated the audience.

I sat up on the sand. The sun was very bright, very hot. I was nauseated. A five-inch gash had been opened on my forehead; I could feel the loose flap of skin, the warm slick blood on my face. The blood had pooled in my eyes and I saw everything through a transparent red film.

Oso pressed the muzzle of his machine pistol against my temple. "Have you got a headache?" he asked. "Would you like an aspirin? I can send sixteen aspirin down this tube."

I coughed and spat blood. The inside of my mouth was cut and I could feel a loose tooth. He must have kicked me in the face while I was unconscious.

Oso's laugh was high and flute-clear. He had the voice of a preadolescent or castrato. Maybe he was ashamed of his voice and that is why he spoke so seldom. And maybe he had turned mad-dog mean so that people would realize that he was an adult.

"You want an aspirin? Just ask me, my friend."

I tried to paste the loose flap of skin on my forehead back where it belonged.

"Show me again how to box," Oso said.

There were bright starbursts of blood scattered over the grayish sand. I read the starbursts as mystics might read tea leaves or chicken entrails—Oso was going to kill me.

"*Uno, dos, tres . . .* " Oso started counting me out.

I knew that I had better get up before he reached ten or he would give me a couple of "aspirin."

" *. . . quatro, cinco, seis . . .* "

The women needed more time to get deep into the forest. And *I* needed more time; maybe Raoul would arrive soon and stop this.

" *. . . siete, ocho—*"

I was on my feet.

"Good," Oso said. "That's *very* good, champion." And he kicked my legs out from under me.

My reflexes were gone and I fell heavily.

"*Uno, dos, tres, quatro . . .*"

I was on my hands and knees now.

" *. . . cinco, seis, siete, ocho, nueve, di—*"

I stood up. And naturally he kicked my legs out from under me again.

Oso laughed with a siren noise and then he began counting again. He counted fast: "*Unodostresquatro-cincoseissieteochonueve—*"

I don't know how I did it, but I was standing when he reached ten.

He grinned at me. "Do you want your aspirin now?"

I tried to wipe the blood out of my eyes so that I could see him clearly.

"Show me how to box, champion."

I swung at him, missed by eighteen inches and fell down.

"*Unodostresquatrocincoseissieteochonuevediez.*"

And somehow I was standing again.

"Okay, that's very good, champion."

I tasted blood, smelled it, saw through it. I had a blurry red-tinted underwater view of the world. Perhaps it was not just the blood in my eyes; my vision might have been affected by the blow to my forehead. I blinked, shook my head, wiped at my eyes.

Oso threw his machine pistol down the beach. "Show me how to box, please, champion." And he slapped my cheek with his open hand. "Like that?" He slapped me again, not too hard, and he laughed. I picked off the next slap with my left wrist. "Very good, champion, very good! " I moved back. He followed and slapped me on my ear, harder this time. I threw a left jab that landed six inches short. My depth perception was off. And I was very slow.

"Show me, champion." He cuffed me again.

I could not think. My mind was fogged, my legs dead, my timing gone. I felt drunk. Oso slapped me with his right hand and I reflexively stepped in and countered with a short right to his ribs, but there was no force behind the punch, no snap. He pushed me away. I staggered backward, fell, slowly got up again.

"What a champion you are!"

I flicked out another slow, short left.

"Yes, champion, now I understand!" And I saw the start of his punch, knew that I could easily avoid it, take a half step in and cross to his jaw.

I was on the sand and Oso was counting. " . . . *quatro, cinco, seis, siete* . . . "

I got up again. I felt better now; Oso's last punch seemed to have awakened me, a shock that somehow partially neutralized the previous shock. That happens sometimes.

"Combinations, you say, champion?"

I jabbed, missed, moved to my left, hooked, missed again, threw a desperate, defensive right and felt the impact on my hand, wrist and forearm. Now *he* was bleeding; blood gushed from his nose. And he lost the sharp edge of his confidence. He was remembering what I had done to him on that other beach on that other day. He recalled defeat. Defeat can easily become a habit. It is very difficult to come back from a beating—your body heals but the mind continues to doubt.

I jabbed him lightly with my left, jabbed again, missed, jabbed and stung him.

"Just what the hell is going on?" Raoul.

Raoul and Dos Santos were standing about twenty feet away.

"Christ, Racine," Raoul said. "It looks like Oso tore off half of your head."

"He's coming along," I said. "Our boy Oso has a future. Hello, Dos Santos."

Dos Santos showed me his beautiful, warm smile. His hair looked like cotton wool in the sunlight. He limped forward a couple of paces and stopped, still smiling. "Bloody but unbowed, Racine?" he asked. His mellow voice had been aged for two hundred years in old oak kegs filled with honey.

"Bloody *and* bowed," I said.

Oso walked over and picked up his machine pistol. I thought about sprinting for the gun, beating Oso to it, and killing all of them, but then I noticed that Raoul was folding his revolver. He was not pointing it at me, but he was ready.

I sat down in the sand. I felt weak, nauseated, but I was thinking fairly clearly now.

"How is my pal Dan Grogan?" I asked Dos Santos.

"Dan is fine," he said. "Just fine. He sends you his best wishes."

I was wearing my cut-off Levis, a long-sleeved shirt, and sneakers. I took off the bloody shirt and threw it aside.

Raoul was very confident: he held his line today as never before; his body was straight, his thin shoulders back, his neck appeared elongated, and his chin was very high. And there was something insulting in his smile and the way he looked down at me with his eyes half-lidded.

I lifted my hand and again tried to press the loose flap of skin on my forehead back into place. And I grinned at Raoul. It must have been a hideous grin, with my bloody face and blood-pinkened teeth and bloody eyes. It was a crazy grin aside from all of that. It was a grin that started in my guts and gathered all the poisons that had accumulated there during these days—bitterness, rage, hatred, contempt—and then rose like bile. My jaws ached.

"Where is the woman?" Raoul asked. My mood, my grin worried him.

"Alicia?" I removed my left sneaker.

"Yes, of course Alicia!"

I removed the other sneaker. "In her tent."

Raoul stared down the clearing. "Where is Sara?"

"She's in the big tent."

Raoul nervously drew back the hammer of his revolver with his thumb, lowered it with a soft click, raised it again. Then he turned sharply and walked down the beach.

Dos Santos was gently massaging his bad knee. He straightened. "Oso," he said. Oso nodded.

I wondered how long ago Dos Santos had recruited Oso: years ago, or days ago, in the camp outside Refugio.

Raoul looked inside the big tent, then hurried over to the other one and ripped aside the weather flap and mosquito netting.

There would be a moment of chaos soon. I intended to dive into the river. If I stayed beneath the water for a half-minute or so, the current would sweep me well downstream.

Raoul trotted back toward us. "They're gone!" he cried. "Racine, where are they? Oso? Jesus Christ, they're gone!"

Dos Santos looked at him with utter disgust; his lips twisted downward as if he had just tasted sour milk. "Oso," he said, and he turned his head and spat.

"Racine, where are they?" Raoul asked.

Oso raised the machine pistol, aimed it at Raoul, and pulled the trigger. Nothing happened. Raoul was slow in comprehending; he stared at Oso, then glanced at Dos Santos. Oso worked the slide mechanism, ejecting a cartridge, bent his head, and blew violently into the open breech. Rust or sand had jammed the gun. Raoul still did not understand.

I jumped up. "Kill him!" I shouted.

Raoul understood then, but instead of first killing Oso, who was armed, he turned and shot Dos Santos four times. All at once Dos Santos's face seemed to compress, flatten, and turn ugly. He doubled over as if with cramps. Raoul shot him twice more and continued pulling the trigger. The hammer fell on spent cartridges.

Oso fired a three- or four-round burst and then the machine pistol jammed again. Raoul finally lost his line: in an instant he reverted to a thin, scared young boy, and then he died.

Oso dropped the gun and drew his sheath knife. The blade was about eight inches long. He was in a half crouch; his feet were squared; he held the knife low, blade up, on a level with his right hip. I moved close enough to draw a strike and then leaped back. He was not too quick. And he sort of hooked with the knife instead of thrusting in a straight line. Sunlight flashed on the blade. He flicked the knife out again, and I retreated. Oso would expect a man always to retreat from a knife. On the next lunge I stepped aside, blocked the hook with my wrist against his wrist, and hit him as hard as I could. He went down, losing the knife. I quickly snatched it up and when I turned he was on me. He threw a big roundhouse right—Oso would never learn—and I ducked under it and instinctively countered with a short right to his heart. The blade penetrated all the way to the hilt.

Oso dead, Dos Santos dead, Raoul dead. The old man, Tono, the ambassador, Brecht, Datone. They had all taken the long count. And maybe Grogan, too. Maybe Alicia and Sara. Maybe me. And no music, not a single trumpet.

There was quite a lot of money in Raoul's wallet and money belt. I took it. It was my money.

I felt as though a very crucial part of my mind was going to sleep.

I got into the raft and rowed out into the river. I don't know why I took the raft; it would have been simpler to walk into town. But I rowed the raft out into the current and that is the last I remember of the next nine days.

I managed, over a period of months, to learn something of what happened to me.

I beached the raft at Porto Pedro on the Brazilian side of the border and hired a bush pilot to fly me to Belém. I behaved very strangely, the pilot wrote me later; I said my name was Cesar Caceras, that I was a member of a film crew, and that I had been mauled by a bear. I talked constantly and cheerfully, the pilot said, although I rarely made sense. But my money was good. We made several stops for fuel. I cleaned myself up and shaved at a restroom at the Manaus airport, and the pilot took some of my money and bought me clothing. We arrived in Belém early in the morning and a few hours later I boarded a flight to New Orleans. That evening I asked to be admitted to a hospital in Houston. I have no idea how I got to Houston, or why I choose to go there, since there are perfectly good hospitals in New Orleans.

The doctors later told me that I was in a coma for six days following admission. They drilled little holes in my skull. And they seemed pleased and very surprised that I recovered with all of my faculties intact. I am a lot more familiar with my faculties than those doctors, and I am not sure they were right.

I remained in the hospital for three weeks. A nurse brought me old newspapers to read.

Alicia made it to San Pedro de los Mártires. Sara did not. Alicia reported that they had safely reached the river that ran north to San Pedro, but then Sara had stopped and refused to go any farther. It was getting dark; Alicia had gone on alone. A search party found some of Sara's clothing on the river bank the next day.

Dan Grogan was reported as "missing." He is still missing. I have a hunch that he will always be missing.

I am now employed by the Los Angeles Department of Parks and Recreation. One of these days I expect to hit the 5-10 at the Agua Caliente racetrack and buy a half interest on a resort in Jamaica.

AVAILABLE MAY 2013

JACKSTRAW

MUNDIAL

I assembled the rifle and secured the telescope to its mounting. The bolt worked with a smooth metallic *snick*. The rifle smelled of steel and oil and wood polish and, faintly, burnt gunpowder. It was the smell of my past, the smell of my future.

At dawn I moved to an open window. A woman, wrapped and hooded by a ropy shawl, walked diagonally across the paving stones toward the cathedral. She flushed a flock of pigeons which swirled like confetti before settling. A limping yellow dog came out of the shadows and began chasing the birds. He had no chance. He knew it; the pigeons knew it. Finally the dog shamefully limped away down an alley.

I went into the bathroom and washed my face with tap water the color of weak tea. The cracked mirror fractured my image into half a dozen oblique planes, like a Cubist portrait, and gave my eyes a crazed slant.

Sunlight had illuminated the parapet and pediment of the National Palace. People were filtering into the great plaza now: churchgoers, early celebrants, lottery ticket salesmen and shoeshine boys, beggars, men pushing wheeled charcoal braziers and food carts. An old man filled colored balloons from a helium tank. Boys kicked around a soccer ball. Policemen in pairs cruised like sharks among schools of bait fish.

Now and then I heard the voices of people passing by in the corridor. A door slammed, a woman laughed, elevator doors hissed open. This was for many an ordinary workday; they would observe the ceremony from their office windows, witnesses to pseudo history.

Blue smoke uncoiling from charcoal fires hung in the air like spiral nebulae. The cathedral's copper-sheathed dome, green with verdigris, glowed like foxfire in the hazy sunlight. At ten o'clock the church bells again tolled, a loud off-pitch clanging whose vibrations continued—like ghosts of sound—to hum in the air ten seconds after the clangor had ceased. Two cops dragged a rowdy young man into the shade beneath the east side colonnade and began beating him with their clubs.

Members of a band were gathering on the steps of the National Palace. Spiders of sunlight shivered over their brass instruments. They wore royal blue uniforms with big brass buttons and coils of gold braid. There were about forty of them and they all looked like admirals.

There was a great cheer as four Cadillac limousines entered the plaza from the north. They moved at a funereal pace. You could not see anything through the tinted windows. Rockets were launched from the four corners of the square; there were prolonged whistles and parabolas of smoke, and then the rockets exploded into stringy flowers of red and yellow and blue.

The limousines halted in front of the palace. Lackeys rushed forward to open the doors. The American candidates, old Hamilton Keyes and Rachel Leah Valentine, exited from one of the limos; the four missionaries from another; and government big shots, in black silk suits and snappy military uniforms, emerged from the other two cars.

The band started playing the country's national anthem. Three fighter jets in close formation roared low over the square, rattling windows and churning the smoke, and when the noise of the jets faded I could again hear the music and the cheering crowd.

* * *

The President of the Republic welcomed the people, welcomed the liberated missionaries, welcomed the distinguished American political candidates, welcomed a new day of national reconciliation and international amity. The crowd applauded. The band played a lively *pasodoble,* "Cielo Andaluz," as if the president had just cut ears and tail from a bull.

The American vice-presidential candidate ended her speech with a series of rhetorical spasms.

"Now!" she cried.

"Ahora!" the dark-haired girl near her repeated in Spanish.

Feedback from the speakers situated around the square resonantly echoed the last syllable of each word.

"And tomorrow!"

"Y *mañana!*"

I crawled forward and propped the rifle barrel on the window sill.

"Forever!"

"*Siempre!*"

I placed the intersection of the telescope's crosshairs between Rachel's breasts.

"All of the people!"

"*Toda la gente!*"

"Everywhere!"

"*En todo el mundo!*"

The crowd loved her.

Rachel Leah Valentine arched her back, spread her arms wide and—ecstatic, cruciform—gazed up at the incandescent blue sky.

I gently squeezed the trigger.

Now. Let it all come down.